BOLD
BEAUTIFUL
LOVE

A TEMPTATION COURT NOVEL

ANGEL PAYNE

BOLD
BEAUTIFUL
LOVE

A TEMPTATION COURT NOVEL

ANGEL PAYNE

WATERHOUSE PRESS

"The way to love anything is to realize that it might be lost."

— Gilbert K. Chesterton

CHAPTER ONE

CASSIAN

A sky of stars. A cushion of clouds.

Heaven is nearly close enough to touch, and it doesn't matter.

The woman I love, attempting to sleep as we fly through the night to the middle of the Mediterranean Sea, is going through hell.

The recall of what sent her there still burns hard in my mind. We'd clutched each other in the middle of a suite at the Marriott Marquis, oblivious to the bustling heart of Manhattan below, as a news report dominated the monitor on the wall in front of us. The images, fed live from the only home she'd ever known before coming to New York with me two months ago, depicted Arcadia island's main bridge as it exploded apart. The river below it had instantly been turned into a mire of floating wreckage...

And carnage.

The bodies of people she'd known. The friends she'd loved.

Soldiers...protecting the country she was equally devoted to.

Including the man who'd been preparing to marry her best friend.

That had been four hours ago.

Fifteen minutes after I'd proposed to *her*.

Fifteen minutes before I'd picked up my phone and ordered this jet be prepared to take off so we could immediately fly back to that island.

It wasn't a decision that made my CIA super spy of a brother—or *her* Arcadian super soldier of a brother—anything close to thrilled. Not that their stress could be blamed. There was a damn good chance the explosion had been orchestrated by a terrorist not even bearing a holy cause for his evil. Rune Kavill's simply a sick fuck who jacks off to the idea of global domination and is hell-bent on acquiring Arcadia as his forward operating base from the Mediterranean. Add the masochistic ax he has to grind against the Arcadian royal family, and the recipe's been right for the bastard to form a dozen shell companies, all disguised as contractors for the infrastructure projects I've been getting ready to start on the island.

Because God forbid Mishella Santelle and I have a *moment* of smooth waters during this wild ride we're calling a relationship.

Or that the world will ever let us think otherwise.

Ella mumbles and sighs. Turns to her side and burrows against me.

Her tawny lashes flutter open—with new tears sparkling on their russet crescents.

I settle to the pillow next to her, brushing red-gold coils off her lush face...the features I've fallen hopelessly in love with. Hers is a face so unlike any other, as if clinging to the past just like the ways of her island home. Until recently, Arcadia was a kingdom stoically committed to old-fashioned ways and a more pastoral lifestyle. In the same way, Ella's face belongs more in a Victorian cameo instead of paparazzi glare—to which she's been ruthlessly exposed since I dragged her back to New York with me two months ago.

Dragged.

It's the word that says too much and not enough at the same time—referring to one of the most brilliant business moves I've ever made, yet the one inducing my harshest cringe of shame. There was likely another way to free Ella from her parents' stifling grip, but at the time, it sure as hell wasn't making itself known, so I resorted to the drastic. Put a number on it. Purchased six months of her life for forty million dollars.

Worth.

Every.

Penny.

No. Not even that. Not anymore. Beyond that.

Far beyond.

The thought sears me as her beauty overwhelms me...as her tears gut me. I'd cut off my balls to prevent even one more of them from leaving her in sorrow—but as more trickle down her creamy cheeks, I must accept that for now, this is all I *can* do. Gather her closer, silently willing the plane to go faster, to get her to the land she loves so deeply...

Ripped apart by a tragedy we still can't fathom.

"Cassian."

Her whisper, a broken breath against my chest, heightens my senses. I smell her, flowers and sleep and the wine I made her sip after we boarded. I feel her, full of nerves despite the Cabernet. I crave her, just as strongly—*stronger*—as the last time she was on this plane and we were headed for the six months in New York I'd planned on using to flush her from my system. I'd been determined to take her virginity, pay her back for the gift with self-confidence to last a lifetime, and then send her into that life without a backward thought for New York or me. My own sanity would be free for the same focus, back to running Court Enterprises with the same single-minded aim on my three-pronged formula for success: taking care of my mother, taking care of my employees, and taking care of my dick.

Three prongs. Simple, right? First rule of engineering: *keep it simple, shithead.*

Well, I got the "shithead" part right.

Forming even three *syllables* seems impossible at the moment, but I manage. "Hey, sweet girl."

Ella rolls a little, peering into the darkness beyond the window. "Where are we?"

"Still over the Atlantic. We will be for a while yet."

Wistful sigh. "All right. I just wish—"

"If I could speed up time I would, *armeau.*"

My favorite endearment from her language causes her to turn back, one hand raising to my chest. "Perhaps I am better off wishing for something else."

I scoot a finger beneath her chin. Tug up. "Like what?"

"Maybe for time to stand still instead."

I rub my thumb over the gentle curve of her chin. "Why?"

She captures the corner of her lip beneath her teeth. Exhales shakily. "What if...things are different when we return?" More tears glisten in her bright-blue gaze. "Not just the bridge and Sancti itself, but"—she drops her stare to the bottom of my throat—"everyone."

"Everyone...like Vylet?"

As I invoke her best friend's name, her features contort.

"Oh, dear Creator!" More of those damn tears fall. "She and Alak...they were everyone's hope..."

"Hope of what?" It's a quiet utterance—probably too much so—but what she needs more than anything right now isn't more tears. She needs fortitude. A wide shoulder. And dammit, I plan on being that shoulder...for the rest of her life.

"That—that it all worked," she rasps. "That two people could be 'arranged' but still find it all. Devotion, connection... love."

I hear her final word but don't comprehend it. Not really. I'm still stuck on the other word in the statement that should negate it. "Wait. *Whoa.* Vylet and Alak are—*were—*" Shit. I hate changing the tense, but the sooner I get used to it, the sooner I'll start getting *her* used to it. "Your best friend, and the fiancé she was bat-shit in love with, were—"

"Arranged." She supplies it with a stunning jolt of pragmatism. Blinks at me, almost angrily. "Yes. By their parents, at the age of thirteen." A shrug hitches at the shoulder she isn't lying on. "It was a little early, but it was also clear to everyone that Vy and Alak were meant to be—"

"A little *early?*" I cut in.

A scowl, edged in more peevishness. "You do know most highborn unions, with the exception of the Cimarron royals, are contracted between the ages of sixteen and nineteen?"

"No." I don't hesitate to match her expression. "I didn't know." But in a strange way, understand her irritation that I didn't. Arcadia is a land in a bizarre state of flux, caught between the security of their old ways and the light speed of a modern new world. Logically, ways of forging marriages and families will be one of the last social components to stick—exhibited by the very situation she was in when we met and the reason I had to act fast with my contracting creativity.

My confession buffs the edge on her ire. She cups my face with a gentled expression. "The only reason *I* was not betrothed years ago is because my parents enjoy diving their heads in the sand." She pouts when my lips quirk up. "Oh, my. How badly did I mess *that* one up?"

I laugh and shake my head. My woman and her talent for butchering idioms is close to legend across Manhattan, though this time I get to say, "Close enough for a backboard shot, armeau. Why did your parents bury their heads in the sand about your betrothal? Better yet, let me guess. They kept holding back for something better?"

She takes a whirl at the twitching lips. For good measure, adds an adorable little roll of her eyes. "Something like that... yes."

I work my head a little closer to hers. Get so close, I damn near bump our noses. "Well. They were smart, then."

"Oh?" Her features flare, a sardonic little move. "Please share, Mr. Court...how is *that* so?"

"They *did* get something better."

"Really, now?" Her eyes flare in mock astonishment.

"Uh-huh." I slant a soft but decidedly sultry kiss across her lips. As we move apart, add in a growling husk, "Really."

"Hmmm." She issues it with more deliberation, knowing exactly how that specific utterance affects me...and my cock. "And I suppose that 'something'...is you."

I let another rough rumble curl up my throat while sliding tighter to her from the waist down. Groan deeper as I slide a thigh between hers, pressing my crotch against her lower belly. Dear Christ, she feels good. The softness to my hardness. The relief for my ache. The kindness and light and passion my life has needed for so damn long...

"Well...I'd never just presume I had the position." A smirk curls up one side of my mouth, betraying how I don't mean a word of it. Thank fuck for the answering heat in her eyes, confirming my cockiness is well-justified—though if I had to fight anyone to earn her, including the pair of social schemers who call themselves her parents, I would summon a whole goddamn army to do it.

But I'd much rather focus on what I was destined to do from the first moment our eyes met.

Love her.

I'm a goner to the cause already—especially as she slants a little glance, blue eyes sparkling, and rasps, "Presuming is never the wisest option, you know."

I tilt my head. "Wise advice from a brilliant woman."

Her gaze narrows. "Now you are just trying to flatter me."

"Now I'm just trying to *compliment* you." I swallow hard, struggling to maintain the charming banter—*not* easy with her silken body shifting against me, tempting me even through my pants and her skirt. "Flattery is for empty words. No words I speak to you are empty, *favori.*"

Her fingers, still against my face, spread wide. Her expression shifts, firming into solemnity. "Nothing about you is empty, Cassian."

The grate to her words is my undoing...and my invitation. I heed both, giving in and moving in, taking her mouth with a deeper sweep of passion, a growing swell of desire.

With a gorgeous sigh of surrender, she lets me in.

Her tongue, wet and warm, dances with mine. Her body, sweet and soft, trembles for me. Soon, a mewl undulates up the length of her throat. I answer with a long, dark moan, not certain if it's in warning or capitulation. Maybe a little of both. Dear fuck, she makes it so hard to think sometimes. When she gives me her desire like this...exposes her need like this...craves me so earnestly like this...

...all I want to do is give her every damn thing she wants...

...all I want to feel is the completion of her soul...

...all I want to hear is the fulfillment of her need...

"*Cassian.*"

Exactly like that.

"I know, armeau." I rasp it while pressing over, rolling her fully to her back. She sprawls against the cushions, where the moonlight bounces off the clouds and glows across the bed. After a few deft slides of fabric, it also illuminates the perfect curves of her bare hips...and the triangle of white lace at the juncture of her thighs. *White.* Never before have I found the color an appealing one for lingerie—if the occasion ever called for it—but for my little Arcadian, no other color seems worthy. She is the purest part of my spirit. The unfiltered path to my light. The perfect start of a joy I never thought I'd know again.

"Oh *my.*" Her whisper matches the slip of the lace as I peel the panties down. Every muscle in my body craves to twist and tear the things free, but right now she needs release and rapture, not a grunting caveman. So I clench everything back as I bare her and then spread her, soothing her back against the pillows the moment she rises up, almost seeming embarrassed.

"*Yaslan riére, armeau. Je yorum conne-toi.*"

She stills. Her eyes widen. I'm usually the one benefiting from the arousal her native language induces. With the tables turned, she's a quivering deer in the headlights...my sexy-as-fuck little Bambi.

"Wh-What?" she finally blurts.

I kiss her again. Take my time, slow and sensual, to part the seam of her lips. Coax my tongue inside the heated recesses beyond, ravishing and taunting and seducing. At the same time, I swirl fingers along the inside of her thigh. Higher...higher...

"Hmmm. What part didn't you understand, beautiful? Isn't *'lie back, little gift...I want to taste you'* pretty clear?"

She swallows. "Y-Yes...but..."

"But what?" I slide her forward, parting her legs wider in the doing. "I've got at least another four hours to prove I was well worth your wait, Miss Santelle...and I plan on putting them to damn good use."

MISHELLA

Well worth the wait.

Dear, sweet Creator. The man would be worth a thousand waits of a hundred years each, even if he never learned all the filthiest bedroom phrases in my language. But as Vylet would say, it is one hell of a hot-shit start.

Vylet.

Sadness knifes my middle. She is one of the largest reasons I defied both Saynt and Damon, the one-two punch of Santelle and Court family protectiveness, to leave New York at once. Thank the powers, Cassian supported my decision before it was even made. He simply knew, as soon as we learned of the devastation in Sancti and the price Vy personally paid because of it, how I'd need to return home.

And there, like a golden chain connected in my soul, is the deepest reason I love him. Am already bound to him, despite our "engagement" being but a few hours old.

He knows me. All of me.

Accepts it. All of it.

The matched pair of dysfunction known as my parents. The cynicism I bore because of them, perhaps the reason why I was more comfortable treating our connection as a contract at first. On the opposite end of the scale, my hopeless naiveté about so much of life in the modern world—the very world *he* helped create with the genius brain beneath that beautiful head of gilt-colored hair.

The head now sliding its way up my thigh, from my left knee.

The golden waves, sending tingles along my skin with every new inch explored.

The bold forehead, striking a match to my core as it pushes at me...right *there*...

"Cassian!"

I do not expect him to relent. Nor do I expect the imperative push of his hands, one on each inner thigh, compelling me to remain open for him.

Surrendering to him...

"I said I wanted to taste you, Ella." His voice is a twist of snarl and seduction, vibrating the trimmed strip of curls that are now the only barrier between his mouth and my pussy. "And you're going to open up...and let me."

As if I need any reinforcement after that dictate, I look down—into the unblinking authority of his green wizard eyes. The man may be crouched between my knees, but there is no doubt to him—or now, to me—who is controlling the lust here. *My* lust.

With that recognition, I know my response has been narrowed to two words.

"Yes, Cassian."

A sound erupts from his chest, dark and low, before vibrating from his lips...which dip between my intimate petals. I shudder, that first incredible contact sizzling through me like lightning, shaking me like thunder. Cassian braces his hold tighter, keeping me spread, forcing me to take the slow, relentless laps of his delving, magical tongue.

It is so much.

Too much.

As my body succumbs to him, my mind threatens to follow. It terrifies me...just the threat of that unhinging, during this hour when so much of my sanity relies on me keeping all the hinges intact. But he continues, exploring my flesh with excruciating leisure, making me feel every exquisite, electric arc of his purposeful, patient licks...

Lightning.

Thunder.

Too much.

I need the damn storm. *Now.*

Attempt to tell him so, digging both hands into the thick decadence of his hair, I yank hard.

Utterly. Useless.

He shirks his hold from my legs in order to grab my wrists. Lifts them with calm but commanding power, riveting me with a newly forceful stare.

"Put them over your head, armeau. Wrap them around the pillow. And *keep them there.*"

For a moment—a long one—I do not move, except to peel back my lips and let him see my locked teeth.

For the same moment, Cassian also does not flinch. By a muscle. Wizard's stare. Warlock's smirk. Emperor's absolution. Royal domination.

He is going to unravel me. And dammit, I already hate it him for it.

And have never loved him more.

With a soft snarl, I roll back. The pillow is a taunting cloud, now puffed a little higher by both of my backward fists, twisting as Cassian laves my slit all over again.

His tongue is fire.

His tongue is poetry.

His tongue is torment, the moment he finds the perfect spark of my storm, and fans it again and again with fresh force.

"Oh! Ahhhh!"

He hums with carnal satisfaction, suckling the cyclone even higher, turning me into a shuddering, quaking twig in the gale, clinging to sanity despite knowing that the end is near...

Sweet *Creator*.

The

end

is—

"*Cassian!*"

And I am finished, thrumming and overflowing, trembling and screaming, rocking and bucking, unable to take anymore—until he gives it anyway, hooking his hands around my thighs and spreading my core like a succulent fruit he cannot get enough of. I moan, wordlessly begging him to stop, but he spikes me into yet another climax, ripping me from the moors of sanity until my body utterly dissolves for him—

Just before my self-control meets the same fate.

It all floods out—the heartache, the horror, the sorrow, the fear—everything I have kept stuffed down since those images from Sancti blared into my brain and tore into my heart. The schism has left cracks. Tiny prison breaks of tears have seeped their way past those barricades, though I have allowed nothing out yet. Nothing responsible for hauling me out like now, into the glare of truth, exposed and raw, naked and vulnerable, open and on fire.

The sobs are wrenching. Exhausting. Freeing. They turn me into a blubbery mess, even as Cassian slides up, unzips himself with alarming alacrity, and aligns his hips between mine. The broad crown of his erection, pushing at my swollen entrance, is already slick with his need.

"Oh...*Creator*."

"That's it," he replies to my gasp. His voice soothes over me while his sex slides into me...fully dominating me. "Give it all to me, favori. Open it for me."

"Cassian." I look away. I am ashamed of the achy shiver beneath my plea, though at the same time, embrace it. In letting go of my walls, I can let in his strength. My ultimate weakness has become his perfect power—a force he returns in every long, hard, determined thrust of his body.

But soon, even he trembles. His jaw hardens, his arms clench, and his buttocks tighten. Every hard, perfect muscle in his body betrays how he holds himself back.

For me.

Yes, he is ready to pour free. But he will not, until I do. I recognize that truth in his eyes—yet so much more too. This all only begins with my physical release. He does not simply want my orgasm. He wants the surrender of my soul, the ache in my heart.

Because he wants to heal the cracks in both.

Like the miracle he is in my life.

"I love you so much."

"Then give yourself to me." He adds a perfect hitch of

his hips at the end of each lunge, causing the tip of his cock to stroke the rare ridge of flesh deep inside, making every inch of my core shimmer in new sensation. "Show it all to me, Ella. You're safe, my love. Let it all go, *raismette*."

And once more, I am completely stilled—paralyzed by a dart of utter magic from his lips. The word, Arcadian for *reason*, is so much more to Arcadians. When a man uses it with a woman, especially with his body buried inside her, it is usually because he is married to her—and pledging his body to hers for all time. Right now, thousands of feet above the earth and hundreds of miles from dry land, it literally has to mean nothing.

But it means everything.

Emotions burst from me...everywhere. Trembling, sobbing, shuddering even harder and higher...

As Cassian empties himself inside me.

He hisses through the climax, baring his teeth in the moonlight. Strains his head back on a groan of primal release. Finally lunges back down, shoulders hunching, as he plunges his mouth to mine, soaking up my sobs with his passion, pulling in my sorrow to every inch of his own soul. No doubt in my mind lingers about it as he drags up with eyes glittering like an animal with a bullet in its side. There is pain there—the kind only possible from a creature familiar with the stuff—but there is also resilience and resistance, born of a resolve to go on. *His* amazing tenacity.

The next instant, his features turn tender. He rubs a thumb across my cheek, his stare trailing after the moisture he wicks away. Presses his lips together to send a hard gulp down his throat. "Thank you, beautiful woman."

I cannot contain a watery laugh. "Thank *me*? For which

part? The first, second, or third time you shot me to the stars"—I nod out the window—"beyond those?"

"For taking me with you to them." He presses his lips to my forehead. "For letting me in. For letting me see all of it. To share it with you."

I unravel my hands from the pillow. Reach them both up to his face, exploring the regal angles of his cheekbones, the bold lines of his jaw. Finally, while brushing the sweat-damp hair from his forehead, the chance comes for my own deep gulp. My throat struggles with it, thickened by emotion. "Thank you for not giving up." Narrowed gaze. Teasing rebuke. "Despite the unorthodox methods."

He flashes a smirk rivaling every sultry male cologne ad in Times Square. "It worked, didn't it?"

I drub his shoulder. "Revelation by fornication cannot always be our go-to plan." I emphasize the point by pushing my face against his right hand—and the newly healed gashes there. "Not always the wisest choice, hmm?"

He sobers and then nods. The memories are still fresh for us both, of the night his own emotional exposure became too much, right after nearly screwing my eyeballs out of their sockets. The crashing emotional walls had been his instead of mine, already tenuous because of the past—and its pain—he had revealed to me that night. Releasing himself physically had torn him apart inside, the price eventually paid by the glass door of his master bathroom shower—and the fist he drove through it because of those violent feelings.

Was that only two weeks ago? It feels like two decades now. We have been through so much. Has it been too much?

And now, we are flying straight into the heart of more conflict.

But we are doing it together. Stronger than we ever were. And bound to each other in a newer, more profound way.

The same conviction glows like fire on emeralds from the depths of Cassian's eyes. He brushes his thumb upward, tracing the arch of my eyebrow. "I know this trip won't be easy for you, Ella." His voice is full of those same quiet flames. "But I'm not going anywhere. I'll be right beside you...through all of it."

Just like that, the tears are hotter behind my eyes. I manage to smile through them, nestling my face into his palm. "I know."

I am capable of saying little else, unable to find any words capable of communicating so much. My gratitude for him. My love for him. My need for him now more than ever, as the miles close between us and a homeland that has, for the last two months, been an unchanging part of my core being...a constant in my soul, despite so many other things that have changed around me, within me.

Now I wonder if anything about Arcadia will be the same.

Petrified about what I shall do if that answer is *no*.

A soft but protesting sob escapes. Despite Cassian's rock-solid solace, I give in to a moment of uncertainty...and fear. Nothing is the same—a truth I always felt myself ready for, until it applied to the constant in my world. Arcadia. *Home.*

A home I will no longer recognize, based on the images from the newsfeed back in New York.

"*Pahaleur armeau.*"

My precious gift.

Cassian's whisper, given from the depths of his massive heart and boundless spirit, is everything I need—and everything that rips me open like wire strippers, exposing the filament of my soul.

I'll be right beside you...through all of it.

The promise settles my mind...but is a restless thing in my soul, rattling the confines of my composure all over again, as a sole question snarls back in return.

What the hell will "all of it" even mean?

CHAPTER TWO

CASSIAN

"Are you fucking kidding me?"

They're the only five words that make sense, in response to the total *non*sense just delivered by Laith—but the guy who's piloted this plane for the last five years wouldn't leave his cockpit to the care of his copilot without a damn good reason.

The message now stamped across every inch of his face.

"That's exactly what they said." Though Laith is chronologically younger than me—yeah, I looked it up once—he often presents as older, with somber gray eyes and an accent hinting at his British heritage. Right now, the frustration on his chiseled features worsens by the second. "I don't bloody understand it, either. We submitted the flight plan before departing Teterboro; the Sancti airport knew we were coming and gave us the ten-four."

I shut the door to the bedroom with as quiet a click as I can. A couple of hours ago, Ella finally fell asleep in my arms; I didn't want to wake her up until it was absolutely necessary. Seems her rest may be extended—and not for a reason I like one fucking bit.

"The tower at Sancti literally told you not to land? For no good reason?"

Laith nods, catching the main cabin lights on the crewcut

spikes of his blue-black hair. Nearby, Doyle sits with a forefinger stretched to his upper lip, indulging in his usual mystery.

"They simply said to turn back," my pilot finally says. "That the landing wouldn't be cleared."

"Wouldn't be cleared? What the hell does *that* mean?" I plunge into the leather seat facing Doyle's. Peer out the window, to where the verdant luxury of Arcadia spreads below. Brilliant rain forests, lush hills, and pristine beaches are accented by towering waterfalls leading to glistening lagoons and sparkling streams. In the distance, the Tahreuse Mountain Range rises and mingles with wisps of white clouds. Over all of it, the morning sun is a wash of molten gold. It looks as storybook-perfect as the first time we were about to land here...

With the exception of the smoke plume still curling from the middle of Sancti.

The remains of the bridge that once joined the city's two sides.

I haul in a tight breath, lungs working in an equally compressed chest. Viewing the tragedy in real life, even from this altitude, is like taking a dunk in ice water. Though I realize she'll likely be seeing it all more closely soon, I'm glad Ella is still fast asleep.

"Damn," I mutter.

"About says it all," Doyle says.

I turn my gaze west, toward the strip of asphalt along the beach about ten miles from the island's capital. "It doesn't look like the airport was compromised, though." *Airport* being a real loose term for this island's thin landing strip, bordered by the beach on one side and a banana grove on the other.

Doyle grunts. "Doesn't mean shit and you know it. There could be a thousand things going on that we don't know about. If those bastards have threatened another part of the city or the airport itself—"

"Begging pardon"—Laith dips a deferential nod at Doyle—"but I don't believe our...*safety* was paramount to their call."

My body rises and my brows drop. "Laith? What the hell do you mean?"

He stares back in open confusion. "Begging pardon again, sir, but I thought *you* might know. That was the impression they gave us, at least."

"The impression?" Doyle slides to his feet now too. "The impression of *what*?"

I hold up a hand, warning him to cut the irritated tone. Laith is, from what I can deduce, an unwitting messenger here—though of what strange message, I still don't know.

Forcing diplomacy into my tone, I ask, "Can you shed some more light on this for us? Remember anything at all, exactly as they said it?"

"Certainly can." Though the moment he declares it, remorse crimps his angular features. "Not a simple thing to forget when a tower uses language like that."

"Like what?"

"Like telling us to 'yankee doodle doo' our 'rich *bonsun* asses' back to countries who like to play with terrorists."

Doyle falls back into his chair. "Fuck. Me."

I push past Laith to pace the length of the main cabin and back. "They've learned something while we were en route. Linked it back to one of our contractors and then naturally assumed Court Enterprises was behind it too."

Doyle swivels. Thumps a fist to the bulkhead for good

measure. "That's a damn huge leap of assumption. You think they'd even *want* to talk to you first?"

Nervous energy bites through my blood, propelling me the length of the cabin again—twice as fast. "They were just attacked, D. The Grand Sancti Bridge isn't just one of their cultural landmarks. It's vital to the commerce of their capital city."

"You spouting that for my benefit or yours?"

I lift a glance suitable for a confessional booth. "Both."

Doyle's glower abates—for two seconds. "So what's *our* new plan?"

Laith clears his throat. "I took the liberty of radioing to Rome. They'll clear a runway if we need one."

Doyle's face turns into visual thunder, reflecting my own shit storm of reaction. I vocalize the tension with a snarled, "*No*," realizing Laith deserves my thanks, not my ire. His statement is the flashlight in the forest, illuminating the only option here. I'm not about to wake my fiancée with the news that I brought her as far as a holding pattern over Sancti Field but turned back with my tail between my fucking legs. *I'm* not the mutt who pissed on the carpet.

"Tell Sancti we're climbing and then holding for a few minutes. Throw some of that Duran Duran drawl into your accent too. Not even dudes can resist that shit."

Laith pinches the bridge of his nose—his version of an eye roll. "And if they ask what the hell we're doing?"

"Tell them we're on the phone with their king."

Doyle pumps a fist. Laith looks like he wants to but only indulges a smirk that does, uncannily, evoke a Duran Duran pout.

I turn from them both as soon as my laptop connects to

the private back line of King Evrest's offices. I have no doubt His Majesty and every last member of his staff are at their desks this morning, probably having never left them all night.

"*Bon sabah*. The offices of His Majesty, King Evrest of Arcadia."

"Bon sabah. Put your king on the line, please."

"*Désonnum*. I am very sorry," the sweet young female on the other end trills, likely reacting to my New York-based number. "King Evrest is not making any statements to the media yet and—"

"That's good, because I'm not with the media."

"Oh." She stammers it out in so many pieces, it turns into a four-syllable work of art. "And may I say who is...?"

"A friend."

"Calling from...?"

"No place that matters on a map." Not a standard one, at least, lending credibility to my tone. Also sounds a hell of a lot better than *thirty-five thousand feet over your island*, since everyone in the country is probably wondering where their next attack will come from.

I wait through the young woman's pause, a few seconds that feel like forever, hoping she doesn't make me pull out my Court-style hammer this early in the exchange. The Arcadian welcome wagon isn't exactly ours to hop on right now. Hell. At this point, I'll be happy with a Radio Flyer on working wheels.

Finally, the secretary stammers, "Errr—all right. Thank you, sir. One moment please, sir. I need to check—"

The girl's own helpless squeal is her interruption, accompanied by a scuffle as if the phone has been yanked out of her grip. Once more, I wonder whether to prepare for a big wagon, a little wagon, or—

"Cassian Court."

"Your Majesty. Thank you for—"

"You son of a fucking lust goat."

Okay. Forget the size of the wagon.

Skip straight to the size of the firing squad.

MISHELLA

My senses rock lazily in concert with the gentle dips of the plane, lulled back and forth between slumber and consciousness by the drone of the engines...

Until a voice thunders, with flawless Arcadian inflection, about lust goats.

I bolt upright. Curl a hand against the center of my chest—and the new sprint of the beats there—while listening to Cassian's response. His cadence is completely him—calm, deep, determined—but completely *not* him, infused with a placating timbre I have never heard from him before.

Cassian Court is *not* a man who enjoys placation. Receiving it *or* giving it.

Another thirty seconds of careful listening, and I am certain the new Arcadian voice is coming from Cassian's laptop speaker—and belongs to a man. A growling, pissed-off man.

Father?

My heart speeds faster.

What on earth would prompt Cassian to call *Paipanne* from the air, especially to be so mollifying with him, and *especially* when we must be close to landing in—

No. Not even close.

We are here.

Despite the confusion tangling my brain, a smile bursts across my lips. My homeland gleams far below, a multicolored gem on a swatch of sparkling cobalt. Not even the mar of smoke can deter my initial thrill at seeing Arcadia again. She is as much a part of me as my blood, my skin, my DNA.

I scramble from the bed, scoop my panties from the floor, and then quickly step back into them. Just as swiftly, smooth my skirt back down. Thank the powers for textured summer skirts made for humid New York City summers—which are a lot like the year-round weather on Arcadia.

Now to lend Cassian some support—in whatever he is dealing with from Father.

Only...

it is not Father.

One look at the tension in Cassian's stance—the taut angles of his shoulders, the sprawl of his fingers at both sides of his lean hips—and I know exactly, even before hearing him say it, to which Arcadian he is really speaking.

"Cassian?" I leave the query at that. There are far too many ways to finish it.

Why have you called the king of my country from the plane?

Why have you not simply waited until we landed?

Why have we not *landed yet?*

Why do you look like a lust goat stampede is about to storm in *here?*

And why are you staring like you wish I *were those goats?*

Seeming to realize the same thing, his eyes crunch shut. When he reopens them, a silent apology glows from the green depths—though the way he reaches out, palm up and fingers curled, is damn near a summons to his side.

I answer it without second thought.

Step to him, sliding against him. Press a hand to the center of his chest, knowing his heart needs the extra fortification as Evrest roughs up the connection with an impatient clearing of his throat.

"My apologies, Evrest," Cassian states. "I was greeting the newest arrival to our conversation. Mishella Santelle has joined us."

"Your Majesty." I murmur it with the respect reserved solely for the Cimarrons while tucking a toe back and bending my knees.

To my surprise, a short chuckle escapes the king. "Miss Santelle, are you dropping curtsies at me from thirty-five thousand feet in the air?"

Cassian chuffs. "Damn straight she is."

"And I suppose you shall turn that into another reason to believe you?" Evrest retorts.

"I don't need another reason, and we both know it." Cassian leans over the work table where his laptop is set up, ensuring the device's microphone picks up every syllable he utters. "I've been aboveboard at every step of every project Court Enterprises has begun in your country. I've always believed in the great things we can accomplish together, Evrest"—he circles his head back, taking me in with a tender glance—"and that was before I fell in love with one of your most beautiful citizens."

"Fell in lo..." Evrest's hesitation is half a second behind the halt of my heartbeat. Even Doyle seems nonplussed by the declaration. The only normal pulse in the conversation belongs to the man with his hand in mine, his grip tight but warm, soothing my knuckles with the pad of his thumb.

"You heard me right," Cassian asserts. "I know it sounds a little crazy—"

"No crazier than how I fell for my Camellia." Evrest's reply brings welcome warmth to the exchange—and my bloodstream, giving a not-so-fun preview of what it will be like to break this "news" to my family.

Saynt will be peeved at first though will warm up given the respect Cassian has already earned from him. But *Maimanne* and Paipanne are the giant enigmas, their reception as unpredictable as what King Evrest faced from the whole kingdom last year when kicking Arcadian tradition square in the teeth. Taking Camellia Saxon, an American filmmaker, as his queen... *Dear Creator.*

My head spins from the concept of it, even now—but the man himself underlines the point with his fresh laugh. "But the heart wants what it wants, my friend."

"Would've called you a fool for that a few months ago." Cassian pulls me tighter, pressing a kiss to my forehead. "Now, I'm the president of the club."

Doyle snorts. Pushes back in his seat. "Just keep those cooties away from me."

In any other circumstances, I would be concocting something to zing back at him. But with more of this scenario snapping into place by the second, I focus all my energy on the situation at hand—and the leader of my country, only accessible via the monitor atop the jet's work desk. "Your Majesty, with humblest respect, you must believe Cassian had no foreknowledge of Rune Kavill's ties to all those contractor companies."

"I'll swear to it in court as well," Doyle inserts.

Cassian slides his hand free from mine. Braces it fully on the desk in order to nearly straddle the laptop with his arms. "I *will* say this, Ev"—his use of the king's nickname, granted only to close friends and Queen Camellia, is a surprise but not a shock—"that asshole is damn good."

Evrest grunts hard. "How so?"

"I mean that my legal team is a group of research sharks. They don't just vet every company we sign contracts with. They dig in, tear shit apart. Reference checks are only the start. There are also thorough investigations of past projects, employee backgrounds, safety records, Better Business Bureau standings... Hell, I think one of their files even included pictures from their employee picnic." He shakes his head, his whole body slackening. "The thing is, Kavill *knew* all of that..."

"Which means..." Comprehension hits me in a sickening rush. "He was a shark about you too."

He jerks a succinct nod. "He knew exactly what we were looking for with every project and then streamlined that contractor's qualifications to fit the bill."

"So on paper, they looked better than everyone else."

"Which is why so many of them ended up on your vendor list." Evrest himself supplies the logical but disturbing conclusion.

"Fuuuuuck." Doyle presses farther back in his seat. His eyes slide shut.

In front of me, Cassian's hands tighten to fists. There is not a single shower door around, though I worry about his laptop screen. My *betranli* is a man of unstoppable conviction, drive, passion, and focus. When those traits are applied to the things he knows and loves—connecting, reconstructing, and improving countries—he is a force of heart-stopping energy, breathtaking beauty. But when he feels helpless and trapped, he becomes a beast in a cage.

"Dammit." His guttural snarl confirms the assessment.

He shoves upright, at least relieving my fear for the laptop screen, beginning to pace a figure eight, hands remaining white-knuckled at his sides. "Evrest...look...I didn't play a hand in creating this fuck soup, but I need to help make it right. In half an hour, you can have me on the ground and in your office, granting you access to every file for every vendor I've hired so far for the Arcadian projects."

My king's heavy breath precedes his answer. "I could also have a lynch mob outside the palais gates, screaming for your head on a spike."

"So keep the peace." Cassian concludes the bite by spreading his arms. "Make me go back to America—and then wait for the weeks, perhaps months, it'll take you to wade through our legal system, subpoenaing those files like our fun legal eagles will make you."

Silence.

So long and so deep, I wonder if the connection to King Evrest has somehow been lost.

Until a few select words of Arcadian trickle through the laptop speakers. Select, as in filthy and furious. I glance at Cassian, wondering if he understands that "fuck goat" is the least of his concerns now.

"You need to give me twenty minutes," Evrest finally barks. "I must find Samsyn." His brother, the spearhead of Arcadia's military forces, is Creator-knows-where in Sancti right now. "Tell your pilot the Sancti Tower will radio him when we are ready for the landing."

Cassian's head drops, heavy with finality, while the rest of his body remains stiff. He is a warrior who has triumphed in a skirmish but understands a whole battle waits ahead. "*Merderim*, Evrest."

My king's snort is harsh, perhaps scoffing, over the line.

"I accept the sincerity, Court, but not the word. In a few hours, gratitude may likely be the last thing on your mind."

CHAPTER THREE

CASSIAN

"By the damn powers, Court. Are you completely demented?"

"He must be. It is the only explanation."

"Creator's balls. We thought that contract stipulation for Mishella was insane—"

"But now *this*—"

"Now, coming *here*, to the palais, while the bridge is still burning—*literally*—"

"Are you trying to be trite, Selyna?"

"Are you snapping at *me*, Fortin? Because if I recall correctly, you were the one who opened us to the liability of his damn contract in the first—"

"*Shut. Up.*"

Every muscle in my body craves to enforce the order by slapping them both—but the dumbstruck faces in front of me belong to Ella's parents. For the thousandth time, I ponder how a pair of such selfish, petty creatures could be the DNA donors for a miracle like Ella. Perhaps she really is the spectral sorceress I have imagined, an angel conceived by the clouds and given to mortals for safekeeping for a while. Trouble is, heaven got the address wrong.

"Shut up," I repeat, gentler because Ella would wish

it that way, and right now my poor woman can't speak for herself. "Stop thinking about the bridge, the contract, or your goddamn liabilities." I turn from where they've been bickering the wallpaper off a Palais Arcadia sitting room, a damp washcloth in one of my hands and large glass of water in the other. "And start thinking about how your *daughter* may need you for once."

"Cassian."

Ella's weak rasp jolts me back across the room, toward the chaise where her skin tone matches the pale damask entirely too closely. The parquet floor trembles beneath my furious steps back to her side. I drop to the flimsy furniture, feeling it shake beneath me. "Right here, favori."

As I stretch the cloth between Ella's temples, there's rustling in the room behind me. More footsteps, as loud and determined as mine, followed by a discernible spike of stress from the pair I've just berated.

"Your Majesty," Fortin and Selyna murmur together.

"Bon sabah." Evrest mutters it as if out of habit, not breaking stride on his way to the foot of the chaise. "How is she?"

"Better." I lift an appreciative glance—all but predicting exactly what Ella does next.

"Your Majesty." Like the good little court employee she's been raised to be, she throws off the cloth and struggles to sit up. "I am fine," she protests—while her head sways and her pallor turns the shade of preschool paste. "Truly. I just need..."

"To lie the fuck back down."

I disregard Selyna's scandalized gasp, catching Ella around her waist—making Evrests's chuckle a welcome surprise.

"This bonsun truly might be the best thing for you after all, Miss Santelle." The king's humor grows when Ella rolls her eyes.

Weirdly, her mother saves the moment from complete discomfort. "Exactly *what* happened?" Even so, Selyna approaches on steps of hesitant caution—only to take over with confidence when I scoot aside, offering her the water glass. As thoroughly as the admission irks me, she may have more success getting Ella to rehydrate.

"We were swarmed by press at the airport. They wouldn't even let her breathe." I issue the statements as evenly as I can, considering the skirmish taking place in my psyche. The fury from once more thinking of that mob, unchecked by any security to be seen, crowding on us with their cameras and questions and shouts. But then the shame for my arrogance, assuming we'd actually be given protection after barely being granted permission to land the plane.

Toto, you're not in America anymore.

Worse yet, a lot of folks around here now think you're the one with the green skin and the bridge-exploding spells.

So much for receptions in the grand hall, state dinners in the ballroom, and fencing matches on the front lawn.

Nothing confirms that more clearly than the entrance of more Cimarron royals. Samsyn and Shiraz Cimarron, Evrest's younger brothers, carry their tension in ways as divergent as their looks. Samsyn, more than embodying his Biblical namesake, is head-to-toe military grit, his black battle gear smudged in mud and cement dust. Shiraz is a different shade of daunting. To-the-millimeter Italian tailoring, shined wingtips, and boardroom arrogance that would daunt guys in some of the highest Manhattan penthouses. Both of them have the near-black hair and bright eyes that have turned the Cimarrons into one of the world's most alluring royal families.

But that's not why they're both intimidating as hell right now.

That I owe completely to their glares at their brother—the fucking *king*—as if he's let a UFO land on their airstrip and I'm the wrinkled alien who's crawled out of it with their countrywoman.

At least Shiraz takes a stab at changing things up. "Cassian." His handshake is, on the outside, a crisp peer-to-peer acknowledgment. Since the day we first met, the same-language kinship has been apparent. But beneath the man's twisted lips and averted gaze, I see the truth. He's as mowed by this attack on his country as everyone else.

I reengage his stare long enough to let him know I understand. "Shiraz." I don't opt for Raz, the nickname he insisted I use during my first visit. Certain instincts—such as every single one in my body—tell me the offer is retracted, at least for now. "How you doing, man?" I'm sincere. He looks as exhausted as Samsyn. Evrest doesn't get folded into the mix. The king's job is to look fresh as a fashion centerfold, even after losing a *week* of sleep.

Shiraz shrugs. Attempts a smile. "You know what they say. Another day in the salt mines."

"Sure."

His gaze lingers longer. I keep my head hoisted, knowing exactly what he's looking for. A flinch, a hitch, even a quirk of regret, confirming I really knew the dickwad responsible for blowing up his bridge and terrifying his country.

Stare all you want, Cimarron. You're not going to find it here.

At the same time, Samsyn has parked his ass on the foot of Ella's chaise. He's still angled over, studying my girl with a rapt expression—a move that'd be turning me asshole jealous right now, if not for the knowledge that Mishella was closer than family to Syn and his wife of just over three months, Brooke Cimarron.

In perfect answer to that thought, the room is filled with a new flare of energy—in the form of the petite blonde who rushes in, bare feet running and long T-shirt flowing.

"Ohmigawd." Brooke Cimarron pushes past both Samsyn and Selyna, sloshing enough water to match the tears spilling from her eyes, thoroughly smashing into my woman. My instinctive lurch of reaction is stilled when a sound erupts from Ella that's pure music to my ears.

Laughter.

"Bon sabah to you too." Happiness rushes to my girl's face, bringing color along with it, earning Brooke fresh points in my book. "Thank you for coming, Your Highness."

"Holy shit." Brooke jerks the compress from Ella and smacks it to her own forehead. "Are we back to that 'Highness' shit already? I'm going to have to bop you, woman. You know I can too."

Ella grins. "Well, I *have* been living as a soft American for a couple of months. Perhaps...you and Vy will need to toughen me up again."

The smile falters as Brooke noticeably sobers. It falls completely when her friend lets out a long sigh.

"Mishella...honey...Vy isn't in a good place right now."

"I know." She bites into her bottom lip. Yanks up her chin, though that doesn't stop it from quavering. "I *know*, Brooke. That is one of the biggest reasons I came back. I need to help her...to get through this."

Brooke takes her hand. "The only reason she saw *me* was because I sneaked in with Syn when he went to deliver Alak's badge and personal things." Her voice cracks into a multi-part sob, joined at once by Ella's. They pull into each other, embracing with that fusion only women can really achieve, as if their souls are meshing into one ball of grief. Selyna watches, a strange confluence of feelings crossing her face, as the rest of us scuff the floor. While we all try to honor the girls' burst of emotion, nobody wants to be personally gutted by it.

Shockingly, the guy who fidgets the hardest about that is Samsyn. After a few seconds of jiggling a knee, drumming steepled fingers, and plotting all his escape routes, he surges to his feet. Instantly, he bores a stare into me. I drill one right back. He jerks his head toward the terrace. I follow him there, dealing with a conflict of my own as we step outside. Arcadia was aptly named. The sunshine is like gold and the air like ambrosia. The admission makes it damn hard to think of someone deliberately setting out to destroy it. *Any* of it.

"Court." From his brusque opener alone, I take a guess where Samsyn is headed with the confrontation. I don't begrudge him the Shao Kahn growl. Though he leads all the security and military forces of this island, the time he's had to deliver personal effects to soldiers' families have likely been few until now. Over the last twenty-four hours, his life has been one nonstop suck.

I turn. Face him directly. "Yeah."

Samsyn locks both hands at his back. The stance bolsters him, firming his expression. "My brother has informed me about what you revealed to him...from the plane. If it is true, you must know that Mishella is like family to Brooke and me."

I lift my head an inch. Samsyn Cimarron may out-bulk me but we're the same height, so the straight-up regard is part of the respect he'll automatically get from me. "It's true," I state with just as much purpose. "I love her. Just before we saw the news report about the bridge, I asked her to be my bride."

The corners of his eyes tighten. "Was that because you knew the report was coming?"

I clench my jaw. Coming from anyone else, I'd answer that by laying him out. Who the hell am I kidding? I still consider it. Instead, I flare my nostrils, haul in a hard breath, and grit out, "No. It was because my jack-hole of a brother had just come back from the dead as an undercover CIA agent, just in time to tell me the three months of vetting contractors for all the Arcadia projects hadn't just been worthless but dangerous." I pivot and grip the balcony rail with both hands, rushed all over again with the unexpected, unnerving fury from that moment. Christ. Was all of that just yesterday? "Ella was the only one who kept making sense, and not just about the bomb Damon dropped. About Damon himself. I almost beat him to a pulp, seeing him again like that..."

"Seeing him?" Samsyn repeats slowly. "Your...brother?"

"Yeah."

"The one who returned from the dead?"

"Yeah."

"After how long?"

"Fourteen years."

"Fourteen..." Oddly, his stunned choke is like a balm. My rage from that moment feels more like a natural human reaction instead of unprovoked violence.

"Long story," I finally mutter. Some tales really are stranger than fiction, as evidenced by Damon's explanation of why he'd let Mom and me consider him dead all those years ago. "Best told over a lot of nectar sometime." I hurriedly add, as soon as my mention of the fruity Arcadian alcohol brings on a Samsyn-style stink eye, "Or maybe a lot of whiskey."

Approving growl this time. Samsyn follows it by leaning on the rail himself, canting a watchful stare. "But he broke cover to tell you about Kavill's game?"

I gaze toward the horizon. This side of the palais angles toward the east, where the airport is situated, but between here and there is a good portion of the city of Sancti. Both of Arcadia's influences, France and Turkey, are evident in the charming architecture that abounds in the white, blue, and terra-cotta structures. The entire scene would even edge into idyllic, if not for the smoke lingering in the air like a funeral pall.

After a long moment of gazing over it all, I finally answer Syn's query. "Sort of."

"Sort of?" he fires back. "How does a career CIA operative just *sort of* come out of hiding?"

"Because it was never his intention for me to find out."

"Huh?"

"Because Mom and I were—*are*—possibly still in danger because of him."

"Shit."

"Because of that, he could only really approach Ella and ask her to help him gather enough evidence from my Arcadian contracts in order to convince his higher-ups to shut down Kavill's shell companies." I shrug, copping to sheepishness. "That was about the point I butted my bitch-jealous nose into the whole thing."

Heavy Arcadian snort. "Ah. Yes. That 'little' monster in the mix."

My one-sided smirk. "Spoken like a man who's danced with that monster before."

"Once. Only my dance was a worse—how do you Americans say it—train wreck?"

"That works. Why?"

"Because my monster came calling *after* Brooke and I were married."

Confusion, party of one. "Wait. *Already* married?"

"Yes. Correct."

"But Ella's mentioned your 'wedding' a number of times to me now—in the *future* tense."

"Correct as well." He pushes back, though maintains his hold on the rail. Squares his massive shoulders. "We shall be saying our vows again—because the first time we did it was rushed and wrong."

I sling a whole smile now. "Fair enough—though nobody would know it from how that woman looks at you."

"The way I *enjoy* her looking at me." Another subtle growl. With the same wolfish surety, he rolls his body over and braces himself backward, gazing through the glass doors at the woman with whom he is blatantly in love. "But when we were first married, it was a thing of hurry and necessity. The Creator Himself was there, of course—He always is—but it was not right...not perfectly so. Words spoken without care are words often tossed from our hearts with matching dereliction." His features, hewn with bold strokes, go noticeably soft. "This woman shall *never* be in doubt about how much I adore her... will always treasure her...and do right by her."

The man has a damn good point. I show him so by emulating his move, turning so the rail is at my back and the view of our women is central for us both. "I like the way you handle things, Samsyn Cimarron."

Even more, I like taking in my Ella when she doesn't realize I'm watching. Sometimes, even now, I know my intense stares make her self-conscious. But how do I stop? How do I mitigate the gashes of her beauty on my soul? Break her hypnotic hold on my spirit? Pretend like she hasn't drilled her life and laughter and vitality so deep inside me, I've been permanently ripped apart and rearranged as a person...as a man?

I don't.

And don't even want to.

The woman has done me in. Killed me off in all the best damn ways—only to resurrect me as a grateful wraith to her voodoo, ready to take on any kind of craziness this existence has yet to throw at me. Yeah, even now. *Especially* now. As long as she keeps haunting all my forms, I don't give a crap what this existence—or the eternities after it—have in store. We're going to face them together, and nothing else matters.

One glance at Samsyn, and I already know he's spinning the same thoughts about Brooke. A soft smile appears through his dark beard before he breaks free with a small jerk of his head. Slides another inspection back at me.

"I am honored by your assessment, Cassian Court," he states. "But know this: I do *everything* right. So if I find out you have lied to us about your ignorance with these contractors—"

"Lied. Right. And *that's* why I brought all their information straight to you on that laptop?" I sweep a hand toward the device, resting on top of the ornate wooden table inside the room—which, creepily, looks like a piece imported from the Holy Inquisitions. "*You*, not even my own government?"

That one sends an impact. No shocker. Samsyn is a

warrior and lives by the codes of such. My action wasn't a step in front of a gun barrel, but it *was* a risk in the name of doing right—and earns the respect now gleaming in his ice-blue gaze.

"Perhaps I like how you handle things too, Court." He turns fully to me, wielding a grunting chuckle. When I respond with a frown, he assures, "*Rahmié,* my friend. Apologies. At times like this, my levity comes at strange times and places."

Curious glance across the terrace. "And this is such an occasion?"

"Would you not say the same in my place, if looking at *your* sorry backside, having to tell Fortin and Selyna Santelle you have proposed to their daughter?"

I grunt. He pretends to cough but chortles into his hand.

"Karma's a bitch, Cimarron."

"But not before you become *theirs*, Cassian Court."

I say nothing. Sometimes, there's just no arguing with the truth.

MISHELLA

A fresh breeze gusts into the room, smelling like salt and hibiscus...

And feeling like him.

Cassian.

The rush of expectancy is no different—perhaps even sharper—than the first time I saw him in the vestibule just a few levels below us. He'd walked in, tall and proud and golden, the sun and wind themselves tagging along in his shadow. He'd blasted through my senses in the same cataclysmic way...

Exactly like now.

Though utterly different than now.

I rise from the chaise, my body responding to our tether of energy. Just like before—only not. Like then, every inch of my skin longs to be flush against him—only now, it *has* been and knows exactly what that heaven is like...exactly what paradise it craves more of. I do not just want him now. I need him.

Also like then, I am conscious of how Mother and Father regard his every step. The push-pull of their assessments—*should we trust him, or should we not?*—only now, reached for utterly different reasons. Instead of wondering how much money they can broker in a contract with him, they are wondering if he had anything to do with the plot to blow up the Grand Sancti Bridge—and how they can leverage more money from him because of *that.*

As the realization hits, the rage does. Rationally, I realize it is the next stage of the fear from what happened at the airport. More logic pounds in the fact that Cassian can more than hold his own with my parents—both at once, even—but dammit, forces beyond logic were what brought him into my life to begin with and what pull me up from the chaise, back to his side, now. As I do, words echo in my head. Oddly, they are those of his brother, given to me just yesterday...

My boy wonder of a little bro certainly found himself a female of quality.

I will be that female now. Prove it to myself *and* Cassian by pressing up to his side, raising one hand to cover the heart I treasure so deeply. "Welcome back," I murmur, lifting my gaze to meet his hooded regard.

"I didn't go very far." That sage smoke enters his eyes, betraying a craving to kiss me, but his stance is stiff, deliberately holding back.

"That is not the point." I do *not* hold back, pretending we are simply back in New York, in our living room at Temptation Manor, and he has arrived home from a long day at the office. As I expected, it unplugs jolts of new energy from Maimanne and Paipanne—though they are different, missing many of the normal threads of disapproval.

"Daughter?" Maimanne steps forward first—of course.

"Yes, Mother?" My purposeful use of the English attracts even jolted brows from Brooke—but I have no remorse about the choice or hesitation about using it again. I used a tone of respect, signifying my continued loyalty to my heritage, but employed the subtle change to demonstrate my devotion to my future.

Father moves forward, taking over the exchange. "We are jubilant to see you, Mishella—and, of course, pleased you returned so quickly." He eyes Cassian and me with even more shrewd attention. "But is the tragedy at the bridge *all* you have returned about?"

Brooke, having greeted Samsyn in similar fashion, breaks from him like a kitten with a fresh ribbon. She circles back around, indeed stepping like a watchful cat, gray eyes wide. "Mishella?" Her syllables are strung together on a good dose of *what the hell, woman.*

Cassian only escalates her agony with a good-natured wink—before grasping my hands like a groom reaching for his bride.

Brooke gasps.

But before Maimanne can, Cassian declares, "Fortin, Selyna...perhaps it's best the three of us speak privately."

His tone does not invite conversation about the matter. Nevertheless, Father mutters, "Yes, of course." Mother mumbles something similar in Arcadian. It occurs to me that the two of them really *are* shocked by the "development" of things between Cassian and me. Can that even be possible, considering they bloody near sold me to the man to begin with?

Pondering the answer to that is not a consideration. As I watch them both leave with Cassian, resignation sets in, bringing a strange kind of peace. My parents have made their choices about their priorities and dreams, but *their* selections don't have to define *mine*. I could swing for the cavalier with the explanation of that—*I've seen the world, and you all haven't*—but even if two months in New York City *feels* like seeing the world, it is not.

And even then...New York did not change me.

Cassian did.

Empowered me with the force of his passion. Lifted me on the wings of his trust.

Transformed me with the magic of his life.

Yes, even all its darkness and the ghosts who live there.

Incredibly, he wants to share that life with me. And I cannot tell him yes too many times. Or in enough ways. Or how much our future together is the glue binding me together right now, jet-lagged and heartsick and still a little sleep-deprived, as sadness clings to the winds of my homeland...

Yet as I watch my man's toned backside disappear around the corner, I want to hug myself from giddiness. *Me*, the staunchest non-self-hugger on earth, wants to simply spin in a circle in the middle of this room and then indulge a nonstop squeal...

Until the option is snatched off the menu by another hug—better qualified as a broadside sack. The squeal is ripped from me too—though admittedly, Brooke gives the duty much better lip service.

"Are you *freaking* kidding me?" She exclaims it while setting me back at arm's length. "Wait. That *did* all mean what I thought it did, right?"

I bat my eyes and bite my lip. "Wellll…"

"Welllll *what*?"

"That depends."

"On *what*?"

Playful chin tap. "Am *I* correctly thinking what *you* probably thought, to infer it meant what everyone *else* thought—"

"Wench," she grumbles as I dissolve into giggles. While dragging me again to the chaise, she chatters, "Ohmigawd. You *have* to tell me everything. When did he ask? And where? And why didn't you call me the *second* you said yes?" She purses her lips. "All right, maybe not the very second, but at least in the same hour."

My laughter fades. I shake my head. "I did not call because three minutes after he asked, Doyle and Damon ordered us out of bed to watch the news alert about the bridge. And then—"

"Out of *bed*?" Saucy waggle of brows. An impish toss of her blond curls. "*Very* nice—as long as he didn't propose while still giving you the New York salami."

I should have known not to go for a sip of water. The straw pops out of my mouth as I choke, "By the bloody powers, Brooke."

"What? Girlfriend, even you know that rule. No fair putting a ring on it while there's still a condom on…*it*." She points to her crotch, waggling her brows. For a woman pale and blond as a Norwegian elf, the woman expresses herself better than a full-blooded Italian.

"Not that it pertains to this conversation, because we

were merely resting on the bed in *all* our clothes, but we took care of *it*"—I use the same motion to rope *my* crotch into the exchange—"quite a long while ago."

She claps her hands. Just once. Very loudly. "*That's* my responsible girl!" Leans forward, eyes aglow like moonstones. "Responsible and...well-satisfied, hmmm?"

"Creator's feet." I slam the water glass down. It is abundantly clear now: rehydration will *have* to wait.

"*What?* Sweet baby Jesus, M, I'm curious. My best friend is getting the naked pony from Cassian freaking Court. Or is he more a stallion?"

My face, likely a mild shade of red before, has to be a lovely dark chartreuse by now. "How do you think I would even know?"

"Because you were just as fascinated as *me* by Vy's dirty internet searches?"

And *there's* the sentence tossing this whole conversation into ice water.

The moment Brooke drops her head, I grab both her hands. Squeeze hard. She huffs, continuing to beat herself up, though we both know the slip could easily have been mine. Cutting Vylet out of our chatter is like taking Rock from Paper and Scissors. It simply does not work.

"We will help her get through this, Brooke." I mold my other hand atop hers. "We will not let her get away with anything else. You know she would do the same for either of us."

Brooke does not say anything. Not verbally. But in her bleak gaze, I read the words she refuses to give aloud. *This is going to take a lot more than a gallon of ice cream and a long walk on the beach—especially if nobody convinces her Cassian was not involved with blowing up the bridge.*

Finally, she rises. Her movement is slow again, almost cautious—but when she turns and smiles, her face is full of nothing but the generous love and boundless friendship she has always gifted to me. "Come on." She extends a hand. "You must be exhausted, especially after the gauntlet you had to endure at the airport."

I dazedly blink a few times before realizing she is right. "Merderim," I stammer. "I suppose...I could do...with more rest." But where? Our departure from New York and our flight here were so rushed, I had no time to think of making any arrangements for where Cassian and I would stay.

"You're coming up to the suite." Her nod is as adamant as her dictate. "Syn and I have tons of room in the second bedroom. You, more than anyone, know that." She hooks her arm through mine. "Besides, we're probably the only couple in the land who won't mind the noise." Fast wink. "We like making plenty of our own."

I stop dead in my tracks. Fitting, since death-like exhaustion creeps over me. "Was *that* a visual I needed?"

"Did I refer to 'visuals' at all?"

"Did you *have* to?"

She poises the other hand on her cocked hip. "Suit yourself. If you'd prefer to stay with your parents..."

I whirl and yank at the link of our arms. "I cannot wait to see the suite again."

She grins and tugs back. "It's been damn empty without you. But seriously"—she stops and sobers so fast, I actually feel my own frown forming—"lately, Syn and I have been fond of the second bedroom from time to time, for its...errmmm... architectural merits. So if you and Cassian decide to take advantage of the toys in the closet, *please* turn up the music so we don't have to listen."

I really do scowl now. "The...toys?" Change out my confusion for a good dose of saucy, as recognition sets in. "My sister-friend, thank you for the offer, but we brought our own vibrator and lubricant, and—"

"And you have *no* damn idea how happy it makes me to hear that." She curls an impish grin. "But I didn't see luggage for either you or Cassian big enough to hold a leather swing or suspension rig."

The saucy was fun while it lasted.

But in better news, things slip into a warm familiarity as I find myself gaping in full at my friend's sex-fiend grin—compelling my hand up, palm toward her. "It is time for you to talk to the hand once again, Brooke Cimarron. The only *swings* I want to know you have looked at are in the baby registry."

"Cart before the horse, sistah-friend." She rocks between her heels and the balls of her feet, letting more glee dance across her fairy-bright features. "Though it's funny, how the 'horse' part still fits. If you saw my magnificent husband just out of the shower..."

"The hand is still waiting, Brooke. The hand is *still* waiting."

CHAPTER FOUR

CASSIAN

I think back on all the movies I've watched and books I've read containing scenes like this.

Opening shot. Two couches, one coffee table. Suitor braced on one couch. Parents watching from the other.

"So. You're in love with our daughter."

Never, in any of those scenes, is that line followed by the one spoken by Selyna Santelle.

"Well, then. Let us talk terms, Mr. Court."

I wish I could say I didn't see it coming from—literally—thousands of miles away. That the second after I asked Ella to marry me, my mind started writing nearly every move of this scenario and then preparing itself for it—which was exactly why I made Ella stay outside. She's had to deal with the uglier side of her parents for twenty-two years, and now it's time for her to stop watching them treat her like nothing more than a sack of rare sugar.

It's not as if the woman hasn't already discerned what's going down in here. At least part of it. She has the most amazing mind I've ever encountered—though how she inherited all this pair's intelligence with none of their deviousness, I'll never know. Nor do I want to.

I'm just determined she'll never sit through the ugliness

herself. Once was enough. Two months ago, she had to sit there like an obedient puppy while I "talked terms" with her parents, as if she couldn't understand every word tossed in the air over her head. My stomach had turned. Didn't take a rocket scientist to see hers did, too.

Mishella will *never* be put into that situation again. So help me God.

If that means staying one step ahead of this pair for the rest of my life—including everything I'm about to lay on them—so be it.

"Now that you've brought it up, Mistress Santelle...let's."

I push back, brushing an imaginary piece of lint off the burgundy brocade of the settee. *Lazing lion*. Ella tickles herself calling me that, though we're usually in much different circumstances when she does. Occasions involving both of us clad only in the bed sheets and each other...

Don't. Go. There. Not right now, at least.

Ella's mother rises. Rubs both hands down the skirt of her linen suit, a dark-pink set with clean lines. She's an arresting woman, though I'm secretly glad Saynt takes after her facial features. The DNA only got passed to Ella in the sun-kissed blond hair and Grace Kelly figure type. "Well, clearly the initial contract has been...modified."

I keep lazily stroking a finger along the top of the settee. Keeps the digit occupied so it's not tempted to join the rest in forming a fist—and then doing something with it. "Modified." Reining back my underline of tension is a little harder but probably wiser. "That's one way of putting it." *And commoditizes your daughter that much more.*

Selyna pivots. Her head bobs on a sarcastic snort. "As I recall, Mr. Court, *you* were the one who presented *us* with the initial contract offer to be the first between our daughter's legs."

Mental file already open: the list of my expectations for this conversation.

Mental checkbox number one: *clicked.*

"Well." I continue stroking the upholstery. *Better than a fist.* If I keep repeating it, maybe it'll sink in. "When one is in an unknown wilderness, always try to speak the language with which the savages are most comfortable."

Fortin grimaces. Sucks in air through his nose.

Selyna stares for a relentless pause. Then bursts into a melodic laugh.

Mental checkbox number two: *clicked,* with a pitching stomach.

Selyna juts her chin. "I may just like you after all, Cassian Court."

I slide a mirthless smile. "Enjoy the party, Selyna. I'll send over a few splits of champagne and cocktail weenies."

Her gaze narrows. "Sounds delicious." She sidles toward the window overlooking one of the palais's interior gardens. The space is elegant and peaceful, and I calm myself by imagining myself out there right now, walking with Ella, our hands twined and our bodies close. Anything except the haughty carriage of the woman strolling before the plate glass now. "But delicious is temporary—and now you are asking for the privilege of having Mishella for much longer."

"Longer as in forever." There's no compunction in my statement—I mean every fucking word—but strangely still feel like I have to *prove* that I do. Christ. This is ridiculous. It's not like I'm meeting with a pair of people who actually care about this.

Correction. About *her*. The woman who means fucking everything to me.

Which is why you're going to finish this out based on your original instinct, not what bullshit the Social Qs have shoved down your throat about this garbage.

"Yes, well"—Selyna laughs as if a four-year-old has ridden through on a tricycle, amusing her with toddler babblings—"we all know what 'forever' can mean in a world like yours, hmmm?"

"Of course." I click off checkbox three while rising to my own feet, borrowing powerful languor from my lion den friends. "That's why she'll sign a prenuptial agreement, even if I have to rope her down to do it."

Fortin stands with a stiff grunt. "Mishella has been raised with a healthy understanding of good business practice." His gaze gleams with tight affront. "But if you *think*, for one *second*, that she would be less than a fulfilling wife—"

"She'll get half of everything I own."

They both go still as ice sculptures.

"You mean...half of everything you *acquire*," Selyna finally blurts. "From this point forward—"

"No. I mean half my assets—as they stand right now and in the future. Period."

Here's the twist I hadn't expected. The two of them, stunned so completely they can't bring a reaction to their face or an utterance to their lips. And this was the part I'd pegged for their next step...

When we got to the best part of this whole damn thing.

"Court," Fortin at last stammers. "Errr...Cassian." His lips twinge as he tries the name on for the first time, perhaps even wondering if I'll allow him. "That is beyond generous. And most, *most* appreciated—"

"Why?" I have to feign the bafflement. *Not* easy. I've anticipated this part too—so much, it wasn't even a designated checkbox.

"Correct me if I am mistaken...but in America, a spouse is usually only entitled to—"

"Whatever is agreed in a contract recognized by the individuals in the marriage and then the state's courts," I supply. "And she *will* agree to this."

"Damn correct she will." Selyna stands firmer. I almost want to slip a whip in her right hand and an amulet in the left, a la Indiana Jones.

"The same way you two will agree to a second, separate contract."

If the whip *had* happened, she'd be dropping it. Her tension spurs Fortin's forward swoop, as if they've choreographed everything to go down like this. But no way in hell could they have predicted my ultimatum. I'm surprised the man doesn't slip in their puddle of drool as they speculate what half my holdings are worth.

Fortin pulls himself up—ballsy enough to look like he's about to add puke to the puddle. "We are her *parents*, dammit."

"Congratulations, Fortin," I murmur. "You can actually say the word. But I won't lose sleep wondering if you know what to do with it as a verb instead of a noun. Or that either of your children is a treasure, instead of a treasure *chest*."

"What in Creator's name is that supposed to—"

I slam him into silence with my vicious turn. Checkbox four—along with the nausea I expected with it. "We're not having that conversation today. I'm too damn tired after our flight and too pissed after the time it gave me to think about why I had to conceive of a separate contract for you two. The truth is, you should be getting *nothing* of Ella's fortune."

The look he exchanges with Selyna, a flash of guilt disguised as a moment of outrage, confirms my suspicions. Every damn one of them.

"You—you are a paranoid son of a *salpu*, and—"

"And you're just a filthy one." I start to pace. My steps make audible pounds. It's either that, or I *will* drive a fist through one of those huge windows. Damn good chance Evrest Cimarron won't be as understanding as Hodge about the damage. "And you know what, Fortin? Paranoia has nothing to do with it. Logic does." I slow my pace enough to ensure they're both listening. "You see, eight hours over the Atlantic gives a guy time to start looking at things. *Closely.* And—surprise, surprise—the more I studied the files of all the contractors I've hired for the Arcadian infrastructure projects, the more I realized exactly what all dirty ones have in common."

"The *dirty* ones? Wh-What in Creator's name are you—"

"Nice try, Selyna." I cut her off with an extended forefinger. "And a beautiful lunge for the kill, especially with Fortin in front to fall on the sword for you."

"I—I have no idea—"

"You have *every* damn idea. Both of you do." I force myself to stop. My next words are too important to muddle with movement. Sole exception: the condemning glower I throw between the two of them. "The only way Rune Kavill could've known exactly what I was looking for on those projects was because he had someone on the inside of the process. And the only way *every single one of them* made it past Court Enterprises' vetting team was *also* because of someone on the inside."

Shockingly, Fortin has the wits to feign his outrage first. "You are making a very large allegation."

The invisible whip returns to Selyna's hand. "Why the hell would we sabotage the advancement of our own country?"

"Why did the Borgias and the Boleyns sabotage theirs?" I counter. "Because cracks in the crown mean holes for snakes to slither in—and take control."

Fortin fumes. "How. Dare. You."

"I *do* dare. In about a dozen different ways." My dead-calm retaliation springs from the control I regain within. No more urges to shatter the window or wear out the floor tiles. "Because *you* dared first." After having my life blown up twice by lies I never saw, seeking the truth is now one of my obsessions—and talents. The shit is as bold as subway graffiti across both their faces. "But right now, the Cimarrons are none the wiser—and any of Kavill's minions who *have* already made it here will be hunted down and caught. The two of you will be kept out of that net because it would shatter the shreds of affection your daughter still carries for you both—and unbelievably, it'll tear her up to see you in the traitor's pit at Censhyr Prison."

Fortin's face pales by five shades. "You would not *dare*."

Selyna bursts with a mocking laugh. "Of course he would not. Besides, the traitor's pit has not been used in seventy-five years."

Folded arms. Calculated shrug. "I guess you trust Samsyn Cimarron's benevolence more than I."

The woman turns the same shade as her husband. After the better part of a minute, she utters, "What are the terms?"

I turn and take two casual steps the left. When reaching the wall, lean a shoulder against it. "You'll receive a generous yearly stipend from the Court Trust, in exchange for *never* pulling this bullshit again with the business dealings of your country. As soon as I marry Ella—and I promise you, that will be as soon as humanly possible—you'll both resign from your obligations and positions in the Arcadian court, using the excuse that you'll be traveling more often to New York, preparing to spend time with your grandchildren."

Only through supreme effort do I restrain a laugh at their first response. Selyna is more horrified about becoming a grandmother than I anticipated—though Fortin is the first to spit words.

"That—that is impossible. I am a respected member of the High Council—"

"I don't give a fuck."

"—and there are *two years* left until reappointments—"

"I don't give a *fuck*."

Silence again. I let it fall. Am even grateful for it. I hadn't lied; I'm toast from the last twenty-four hours, and pretending I'm not rejoicing in every second of this is an even deeper drain.

Especially because I'm not even done yet.

"You'll have plenty to stay busy with, Fortin." I drain as much of the sneer from it as I can. "Take up golf, man; I hear it's fun. Go catch some Pokémon, or have fun investing your money the *honest* way. You'll only have mine for a limited time anyway."

That certainly perks Selyna up. "Excuse me?"

"Ohhh, right." I snap my fingers. "Forgot about the fine print, didn't I?"

Her glare darkens. "*What* fine print?"

"You see, the fund for your stipend will be dissolved and distributed to a number of drug rehab nonprofits upon my death. If that death 'just happens' to occur sometime soon and is deemed to be at all suspicious, my legal team already has instructions to unseal the contents of the file I wrote up during the flight. In it is all the information they need to share with the Arcadian *and* American authorities—connecting the two of you, in some shape or form, to every single one of Kavill's shell companies." I hitch a corner of my mouth. "Remember, all those contracts were executed in New York City. So if, by some weird circumstance, they've turned the traitor's pit into an herb garden, we have a few fun tourist spots for you to visit in the States too." Finally, I push from the wall. "You'd rock an orange jumpsuit, Selyna."

For at least three minutes, the only sound in the room is the peaceful cascade of the waterfall out in the garden—a clash to the gears I imagine grinding in both their heads.

In the end, it is Fortin who fortifies his stance—but that isn't the most surprising twist of the moment. That comes in the form of his glare, burning at me with the force of a pale-blue flame thrower—

The exact same color as his daughter's.

"Send your fucking contract, Court."

I push up from the wall. "It's already been emailed, sir."

"Fine. Now get the hell out of my sight."

MISHELLA

The sun is warm, the breeze is light, and I'm running on the beach, holding hands with Vy and Brook. They trade sarcastic Americanisms, and right now, I am too happy to even care.

The sea washes over our feet, leaving foam that sparkles like crystals in the sun. I look down at it and see a shell lined in the most incredible, iridescent shade of green—like Cassian's eyes.

I need him.

And just like that, he is there.

Rivaling the sun. Defying the power of the air itself.

I hand him the shell, and he smiles, tucking it into the pocket of his white shirt, which is unbuttoned all the way, revealing his sculpted pecs and rippled abs. Samsyn and Alak, joining hands with their women, are dressed exactly the same way—

No. They are not.

Alak...is not.

His shirt is red.

Stained that way...from blood.

Blood that will not stop.

It flows and flows, the stain growing and then the blood dropping, spurting across the sand and then spreading into the sea, before he turns to walk into those crimson waves. Vy sobs, reaching for him. Screaming for him. But he does not stop.

And then is followed by Samsyn...

then Cassian.

"Nooooo!"

My shriek jerks me to consciousness between my lungs' frenzied pumps. I bolt up in bed, scraping a hand back through my hair, staring around wildly.

Before I can kick the covers free, massive muscles band around my waist. "Ella." There is not a note of sleep in Cassian's voice, though he was more exhausted than I when we finally fell into bed, lulled by the crashing waves on the shore just beyond the terrace.

Or was he?

Was all of *that* just a dream too? Maybe we are still back in New York and everything from the last forty-eight hours is just a massive, crazy tangle of my imagination...

"Ella." He lifts a hand to my hair, pushing it off my face. "It's all right, armeau. Ssshhh. I'm here."

I swallow hard as the last tendrils of sleep fall away. "Wh-Where are we?" My head lifts as a wave slams the sand outside. "Oh."

"Oh?"

"It was not a dream, was it?" A sob bursts free. "Even the part about Alak." The images invade my mind, so vivid now. "That—that means—" Even the part about Cassian following Alak into the water. "Oh!"

Cassian grunts as I twist, launching myself against him. He reacts quickly, easily absorbing my weight and then wrapping me close. "Hey...whoa. Ella...baby..."

"Do not let me go."

"As long as you breathe for me, okay?"

I comply with a long breath. Twist desperate fingers into the ends of his hair. Find myself eagerly indulging the next inhalation, since it is filled with the sandalwood and ocean scent of him. I suck in another, letting it inundate every corner of my senses—though it does little to help the weak squeak of my voice. "Do—do not leave me."

He answers before a beat can go by. "Never." Tightens his hold until his fingertips clutch opposing sides of my rib cage. "*Never.*" After we are like that for a few minutes and our heartbeats slow in tandem, he murmurs, "Want to talk about it?"

I keep my death grip—dear powers, what an awful expression—on his neck but slide my head back so he can see me shake it. "I just...really need to find a way to Vy."

He nods as well. "Okay."

I try to let it reassure me. When this man gives his word,

he means it. His hundreds of business partners and thousands of employees know it. *I* know it.

My heart is still troubled. Off-balance.

"We were only girls when we met, Cassian. Twelve. In this horrid class where we had to...*run laps.* I hated it. I was so bloody formal and serious—"

"You don't say."

I tug on his hair to retaliate for the tease. "She was so... everything I was *not.* Sassy and funny and beautiful..."

He loosens his hold in order to slide a finger forward, pushing up my chin. His gaze is waiting for mine, intense as the fireflies dancing over Sancti Lagoon. "Do you really *not* see how you are all those things too?"

Heavy breath. "Because Vy taught them to me."

"Because they were inside you all along." He raises the other hand to the side of my face. "Vy just granted you the freedom to show them to the world."

I gulp again. Soak in his words as the precious truth they are. "But now she refuses to let *me* in to help *her.*" Vocalizing it is supposed to help...but the conflict in my chest just cracks open wider. Out of that fissure, tears escape. Not a huge flood, for this sadness is more crushing than that. More soul deep.

"Everything is so different now, Cassian..." I turn my gaze out toward the terrace. The moon on the waves is like the diamond bracelet on my wrist: a representation of so much more than refracted light. In the waves, the moon finds magic. In the circle of my bracelet, there is a symbol of this man's unending love. Even now, in the middle of the night, he waits for me with quiet but alert patience. I have to find more words for this...to give him. "I have come back here, feeling so much stronger than when I left..."

He cups my shoulders and squeezes. "Because you *are*."

"Then why do I feel so damn helpless?" I hate the pathetic rasp of it. Even more, I hate the bitter truth of it. "What have I returned for, if I cannot assist with anything?"

"Favori." He kisses me gently. "It's temporary. You know this. The situation on both banks of the river is chaos right now. Samsyn isn't even allowing Brooke to go down there, and *her* bad ass still works for him."

I pout. "*I* am badass too."

"Damn straight you are." He adds a growling undertone, injecting the leonine energy into his next kiss. "But you still can't traipse around Sancti without a security escort. Not right now. Things will start to normalize as soon as Evrest addresses the country on the news tomorrow."

Rough huff, take two. "So...I am just supposed to sit around here, watch the flowers grow, and have my nails done?"

He dips his head, capturing my left forefinger between his playful lips. "Your nails are beautiful, just like your huge heart."

"I do not want to be beautiful. I want to be *useful*." My words are now close to pleas. They agitate me, driving me off the bed. Here, in the land which has always meant *home*, the only thing feeling close to that is literally the shirt on my back. Cassian's faded Fordham U T-shirts have become my sleepwear of choice—when the situation calls for things like that. "But I cannot rebuild a single strut of that bridge. I cannot bring back Alak for Vylet. And I cannot step foot outside this palais, much less help Samsyn in the hunt for those bonsuns responsible for all of this!"

I halt in front of the open terrace doors. Breathe deeply again, all but ordering the ocean wind to permeate my rioting spirit. *A* for effort; *F* for success. The refrain is becoming all too regular in my life.

Helpless, as that thug in Bryant Park unloaded three bullets into Cassian.

Helpless, waiting for Doyle to arrive after Cassian punched out his shower.

Helpless, watching the Grand Sancti Bridge get blown apart by a terrorist's bomb.

Helpless, standing here, beholding the beauty of a vast, sparkling sea—unable to let any of its glory into my grieving heart.

I hunch into myself, ordering the pity party to stop. It just seems to get worse...

Until Cassian presses up behind me.

And the very air I breathe is altered. Empowered. Made better simply from the force of his presence...the power of his warmth...the subtle shift of his mien. The very pores of my skin drink in his new energy, absorbing the sizzling lava flow of his intent.

I sure as hell am no calmer now. But for much, *much* different reasons.

"I know a way you can help Samsyn." He utters the words into my hair while skimming his fingers along my shoulders, down my arms. I do not hide the shiver he induces...how he wakes up every inch of my body simply by raking his touch over me.

He trails fingers over my hands and then underneath, lightly scratching my palms. The contact zips fire back up my arms and then inward, tingling my breasts...punching into my nipples.

"Oh?" I battle just to get that out. As the magic of his touch takes over, I forget where I am...while never being more aware of everything around me.

"Mmmm hmmm." His rumble resonates through us both. He steps closer, sliding his feet against the outside of mine. Nearly molds himself around me... "By keeping *me* sane."

"That sounds..." I gasp as he twists fingers into my hair... and then uses the grip to tilt my head to one side. "Like an interesting proposition."

"We call it indirect procurement." His lips move along my neck with smooth, seductive intent. "It refers to valuable... services...that benefit internal stakeholders to an organization, so they are empowered to help clients better."

My eyelids grow heavy. The feeling settles through my muscles before throbbing deeper, gathering into a hot lead weight in my sex. Dear Creator, how I want him... "And I am such a...procurement...for you?"

Cassian's lips part. His teeth nick the skin beneath my ear. "Best fucking asset I ever added."

His voice is a rough rasp. His words, filthy and possessive. As the strong woman he has helped me become, I should be considering how best to circle and slap him for them—but as the woman he has fallen in love with, I absorb them, crave them. They are his worship of me. His pledge to always bring me everything I need, crave, desire...

Which, when all is said and done, only circle back to one sole thing.

Him.

Surrounding me with his heat.

Melting me with his touch.

Roping his way into my mind with all his illicit words...

"So will you service my...internal needs, armeau?" It is fire in my ear...and then every shred of my nervous system.

"Empower me so I can help Samsyn in every way that I can?"

"Yes." I hear myself say it through the haze he swirls and thickens over my senses...my body. "*Yes*, Cassian."

A slow growl emanates from him. "Will you give me all of this?" He drags his free hand beneath the T-shirt, exploring my belly, my rib cage, the erect points of my nipples "And all of this?" Descends that hand, dipping into my panties, cupping my quivering mound.

"Yes," I breathe. "Oh, Cassian..."

"Uh-uh." He pinches my inner thigh, making me yelp. "You're the asset now, Miss Santelle. That means you'll refer to me as Mr. Court." A swift pinch on my opposite thigh. "And you'll give me exactly what I want right now."

Oh, dear *Creator*.

He does truly know me.

Every depraved, dirty, filthy, feminine corner of me.

But best of all, he will not hesitate to fill me there.

Beginning this moment.

With a harsher coil of his hand in my hair, he angles my head up and back. My eyes flare open, succumbing to the surprise of it—and the glory of the submissive pose he has invoked. My vision is filled by his face, hard angles and burning lust branded onto his tawny skin, surrounded by the sleep-tossed mess of his hair.

By all the saints, he is beautiful.

And perfect...

With his mouth descending.

His tongue invading.

His fingers still tightening against my head. Hurting...just enough to make me moan and widen, letting him explore my mouth in deeper plunges of passion, hotter sweeps of heat I cannot and will not deny...

"Oh!" It spills before I can even get air back in when he finally pulls back. The edges of his lips quirk, followed by a gleam in his eyes that cannot be mistaken. The lion is already proud of his kill, and his feast has barely begun.

And the prey could not be happier.

"You liked that, hmmm? Answer me," he prompts when all I give is a wobbly nod. "And remember how to do it, girl."

"Y-Yes, Mr. Court. I—I enjoyed it. A great deal."

"Good." His stare lowers, taking in my whole face with thicker regard. At the same time, he snags his lower lip with heart-halting slowness. "Because I have *much* more to give you."

"Th-Thank you, Mr. Court."

I have no idea if it is the right thing to say, though the fresh spark in his eyes is encouraging. Exhilarating. My breath catches all over again in my chest. *What is going on?* This is different than simply anticipating a good fuck with him. Yes, *that* part is always good.

But this...

Is different.

There is something new here. New...to him. And...to me.

Is it the island? This room? The constant adrenaline we have both been subsisting on, due to what brought us here?

And do I really care?

I only know I love the feeling of it. Every frightening, heart-halting moment of it.

Even as he slips his hands free from me—pulling the T-shirt up and over my head on the way. "Lose these on your way to the bed." His growled instruction comes with a flick at my lacy panties. "Then lie down on the side of it with your head down and your sweet bare ass raised for my pleasure."

I swallow hard.

"Yes, Mr. Court."

Set the lion free.

CHAPTER FIVE

CASSIAN

She is a dream.

She has to be.

I had no choice about falling in love with her—my soul told me that from the second our eyes met—but right now, I officially worship her. Long to fall to my knees as I kiss the backs of hers and then slowly make my way to her toes, kissing each in utter gratitude, confirming she is, in fact, a complete reality.

But I can't do that right now.

Because of this gift she is openly giving me.

Her nudity. Her vulnerability. Her trust. Herself.

"Good girl," I praise, shocked about the paste glob my mouth has turned into while stripping from the cotton shorts I was sleeping in. Commando's my usual preference, but we're houseguests in a land still on high alert, inside a guest bedroom with a non-locking door. Not that I'm worried about Syn or his little bride intruding. Earlier, the man himself pulled me aside to make sure I knew about *all* the amenities of our accommodations—including the fact that the closet doesn't just contain extra clothes hangers.

The closet I now step to and slide open.

"Cassian? I-I mean...Mr. Court? Wh-What are you—"

"Miss Santelle." It's threaded with calm and command at the same time, compelling her head back to the bed's gold coverlet. "Do you trust me?"

I swear to God, her quiver shakes the air. And then, in a sublime rush, her surrender. "Yes." Her declaration is proud. "Yes, I do."

"Then you'll continue doing just that, won't you?"

"Yes, Mr. Court."

The next few minutes are among the most silent—and electric—of my life.

I'm not a card-carrying member of any wild and kinky "scene" but have dated enough members of some to know my way around a spreader bar. But while the equipment is familiar, absolutely nothing about the rest of this is. She isn't just another moaning female, ready to take as much from me as I do from her. I'm not just a horny prick searching for an interesting spike in my sex life, something to distract me from the noncommittal biology that's about to happen. This is...energy exchange. Deepening trust. The gift of her body to mine. The relinquishment of her personal will—a commodity that has, for so much of her life, been the only thing she can rely on.

"How are you?" I ask it while once more testing the snugness of the leather cuff around her right ankle. The O-ring at the back of it is latched into the connector at the end of the steel bar.

"I am...good. Thank you, Mr. Court." Her voice is a husk of lust, punching straight to the core of my cock. Christ. I haven't even started to push out the bar yet. Her pussy is still just a peek of pink—and her ass isn't close to what I crave.

What I have planned...

"That is very good to hear, because we're only getting started." I finish that by twisting the pin free from the middle of the bar. "But before we do, you need to tell me that you understand two things."

"Of course, Mr. Court."

I stroke her thighs from ass to knees, literally caressing more security into her. "Number one: I am going to open you, Ella. Touch you, and then fuck you, in ways we've only talked about before. Push you...in order to plunge you into deeper bliss than you've ever imagined. To do that, I don't just require your trust. I demand it."

A heavy swallow rolls down her throat. Her shoulders bunch up and then visibly soften. "You have it." And suddenly, her voice is strong and clear. "I promise."

"And your promise leads to point number two. *My* promise. This isn't some game, Ella. Nothing between us will ever be a game. So if you say no—if you even whisper *stop*—that's my complete sign to do so. Got it?"

She's listened to my declaration in such stillness, her playful little wriggle comes as a strange precursor to her surprise of a reply. "I would not dream of ever asking you to stop, Mr. Court."

Well.

Two can play at *that* teasing game.

And I do—in the form of a sound that's half savoring snarl and half wicked chuckle.

"But you have no idea what I am going to ask of you, Miss Santelle."

MISHELLA

The shivers deepen with every new clink of the bar.

Tremors along my skin...expanding through each of my pores...and then claiming every fiber of the flower at my core, unfolding for his gaze...exposed even more when he turns on the bedside lamp and even removes its shade.

"Fuck," he rasps. "Fuck. *Me.* You're so perfect, Ella."

A blush crashes in, along with my shivers. The sensations are a skirmish in my senses, causing my muscles to react, instinctively wanting to hide. But I cannot. I am his. Controlled by him. Submitted to him. Offered to him...

Open to the fingers he slides over my trembling mons... and then through my wet, achy slit. A prisoner to the jerks of my body, trying to push at him for more...but needing to escape the intensity...

He seems to know this and pulls away.

Only to pull that damn pin again.

And spread the bar wider.

"Ohhhh..." It stammers from me as a cool wind brushes in from the terrace, caressing the exposed nub at my core and all the aroused folds around it...

And now, the sensitive rose of my backside.

I am spread so wide, even those delicate edges are now bared—a fact not escaping Cassian's attention for a moment. From the dark satisfaction in his new growl, I might even guess this has been his purpose all along.

I am going to open you...touch you, and then fuck you, in ways we've only talked about before...

"Oh...*my.*" It is not such a stutter anymore. The fear will not allow for that.

Cassian pauses, his hands spread across my upper thighs. "That's not a stop."

I force moisture into my mouth. "No, Mr. Court. It is not."

"Then grip the bed cover, Ella. And push against me."

Push against me. He has used the words before when exploring the tight tunnel of my backside—even when plunging his fingers there while taking me with his cock—but there is a new element in this version of his command. A guttural catch, as if resonating from his deepest self...the root of his whole essence.

The cock, like velvet steel, he slides between my ass cheeks.

Without hesitation, I curl both hands into the comforter. *No games.* If he means it, I am going to need the security.

My grip tightens as he rubs everything along my crack— balls, shaft, crown—over and over and over again.

Tighter as he lays a stream of lube between our flesh.

Tighter still as he reaches down—and breeches my pussy with his fingers.

"Oh!" I must be setting a record for the utterance tonight, but it is all I am capable of. "By the Creator!" Or...maybe not. "What—*what*, by all the saints, is—"

"Relax, sweet girl." He tosses the lube aside to keep my lower back pressed all the way down. Why does his voice sound so labored...and so sexy? "Just push into it."

Push into it. Right. Only with what...and how? As his cock continues to tease at my backside, the lube slicks over his separate invasion, stretching the walls of my other entrance. It is not his fingers, nor the bullet-style vibrator he sometimes likes to use on me. This...*thing*...is as big and long as his penis, only it is hard, unrelenting...

And vibrating.

"Dear...*Creator.*"

It bursts from me, half scream and half choke, as every inch of my core is turned into a conflagration of stars battling into my bloodstream at once. As soon as it does, my body sizzles into a state that proves every syllable of his promise true. I have never known bliss like this—only in the same moment, it is torture, giving way to the need for more. In the space of ten seconds, I am his sensory addict, shrieking from inexplicable arousal...begging without shame for more.

"Is that good, my sweet armeau?"

"Oh...oh, *Cassian*—"

"What?"

"I—I mean—Mr.—ummm—" Hell. What is his name? What is *my* name? Do I care? Do I need to care? "Oh—*dammit*—just do not stop. *Please* do not stop!"

I am shaking so hard, the spreader bar rattles. Cassian twists, working the device deeper into my pussy. I groan, torn between ecstasy and elation. I have never wanted to climax more in my life while craving to be held off...shown to higher precipices.

He backs off.

I moan in thanks...and hatred.

"Sweet...fuck," I gasp. "Oh...*please*..."

The vibrator is in tight. Cassian leaves it there, now using both hands to widen my ass cheeks. Cold liquid penetrates deeper into my most forbidden opening. His fingers slide in, pushing me farther and farther apart...

Taking turns with the head of his cock.

The sensation is...

Full.

Immense.

Too much.

But not enough.

Something inside me craves more. Needs this push over the edge of anything I've ever experienced before...this gift of everything in my body, my mind, and my soul to him. Letting him command everything he needs. Letting him claim everything he wants.

Letting him fuck everything he wants.

And still, I feel him holding back. His own body betrays it, coiled and tense as he starts to work at my rose with his cock alone. But not *all* of it...

Until he digs a hand into the flesh of my hips. Uses the other to work the vibrator high and hard into my sex again. Groans and purrs at once, starting to set a wildcat rhythm with his hips.

My body throbs and rocks, attempting to meet his thrusts. With what few brain cells he has not yet pounded from my skull, I focus on keeping my muscles open and expanded instead of clenched and climaxing. It is *not* easy, especially when he clicks the sex toy to a higher setting. Slicks everything with a fresh coat of lube. The contrast of the cold liquid to my hot...*everything*...adds another layer of arousal to the mess of my senses.

"So...good," I manage to pant out. "So...damn...good!"

His snarl is a raw, low coil. His hold is a brutal, hard demand. His thighs are flexed sinew between mine, meshing his sweat with mine. The scent of it is thick in every electric ion of the air between us, intensified by the gusting wind across the terrace. "You want more, Miss Santelle?"

"I...I want more, Mr. Court."

"I've never been happier to hear that."

The vibrator whirs higher. The spreader bar jangles louder. The wind rushes in.

As he surges his body fully into mine.

I scream. Nearly rip the comforter. Pain slams me—but so does a wash of want so full and sharp and raw, it is part of the same blast. My whole being is a sudden, massive storm, beauty and violence and destruction and redemption bursting as one fierce, fluttering entity—especially as my sex implodes with ecstasy, my body ignites with fire, and my senses shatter into silver-white nothingness. As I come, Cassian intensifies his grip, locking our bodies. His balls, caressing the secret flesh between my pussy and ass, do not take long to constrict and pull tight—making his cock pulse and then expand.

With a ferocious groan, he climaxes deep inside my body. I am filled with his hot essence. Immersed in his dark passion. Claimed by his flowing fire.

Covered in his rough praise.

"*Douli favori. Douli kupette betranli. Ma dinné.*"

Sweet special one. Sweet little betrothed. My woman.

Words for every part of me.

Love for every need in me.

He repeats it all while gently pulling everything out and then unlatching me from the bar. Through it all, I barely move. My body is a puddle of pleasure, my mind a fuzz of numbness. For the first time in nearly two days, no thought will stick to my mind for longer than a few seconds—and it is complete paradise.

I stay prone while Cassian rises and then disappears for a few seconds. Nearly to the second he starts running water in the bathroom sink, rain begins to patter on the terrace. Unlike the tempest still calming inside me, the drops are a simple, gentle midnight shower. Even the accompanying thunder is just a scrape against the air, adding to the utter calm permeating me. If the rain can still fall and the skies are still moving, perhaps the world has not changed as traumatically as I have dreaded.

Perhaps Vy will let me back in and help her heal.

Perhaps, in a little bit of time, Arcadia will unite and recover too.

Perhaps, after the pain, we will all be a little stronger.

The hope is as warm and comforting as Cassian's return. He brings a wet cloth and uses it to clean me with tender, quiet strokes. He stretches out next to me, not making any overtures to turn me back over. As if my reverie is a glass bubble, he does not disturb it beyond the light strokes of his knuckles down the slope of my back.

For a long time, we are wordless but full, content with no sounds occupying the air except the rain and our breaths. But I watch him. Am mesmerized by him. The play of the watery shadows over his chiseled forehead, long nose, strong chin. The gleam of lightning flashes in the jade striations of his eyes. And after a few minutes, the mystery of the smile at one end of his elegant mouth.

"What is *that* for?" My whisper hints at amusement.

His brows lower. "What is what for?"

I poke the corner of his smile. It triggers the subtle lip-twisting thing that brings out his dimples. *Creator, just give this man the rest of my heart now.*

"I was just thinking..." His mouth contorts even more, making me frown now. He is genuinely troubled. *Shit.*

"Thinking? About what?"

I lick my lips, not shy about the nervousness. As his gaze

follows the motion, his expression darkens.

"Thinking about *what*, Cassian?" I hitch up, resting my head on an elbow. "Or is it still Mr. Court?"

My belly skitters in more distress when even the humor does not lighten him. By the time he finally forms a hand to the curve of my waist and takes a long breath, my heart thuds through the beginnings of fear.

"Even if *I* looked at Mr. Court in the mirror right now, I wouldn't recognize him." His frown changes again. Deepens... though in a way that my stomach stops flipping, in favor of my heart aching.

"What do you mean?"

He rolls his thumb against my skin in a circular motion. Rubs his toe along the top of my foot in the same cadence. "A person...changes throughout their life...you know? You've got childhood and then getting through school...and then figuring yourself out in college...but by the time you think you've got *that* figured out and you're ready to be an adult, the whole process starts all over again. Slap a few acronyms after your name on the office door, and that doesn't stop any of it, either. Life just catches up. Slaps you in the face. Humbles you when you least expect it."

"Like bringing your brother back from the dead?"

"Only to have him tell you that you've gotten into professional bed with a psychotic terrorist?" His strokes speed up for a few moments, until he takes in another huge breath. "Yeah, shit like that."

I reach up. Slide a reassuring hand over the firm expanse of his sternum. "My. You *have* been thinking."

He dips a quick kiss to my knuckles. When he looks back up, there is new light in his eyes. A fresh rush of thought across his features. "The tidal waves...they suck. But in a way, they're miracles. They force you to remember who you are...maybe, perhaps, to redefine that person a little." He shrugs. "Or a lot."

I attempt to smile. Another *F* for achievement. I am sure he sees my confusion now too.

"Then...there's that creature, the essence of who you are, that doesn't change at all," he continues. "That primitive, essential force, deep inside... Hell, I don't know; maybe that's what everyone calls the soul...but it's just there, ultimately driving you, right? And...you know it's never going to change, so you beg heaven to bring you just that one person who sees that...and gets it. And doesn't just get it but loves it. And you also beg heaven that if it's that bountiful with the blessing, you'll be paying attention enough to see that you've been given that one...and that you'll hang on to them like a fucking bar of gold."

Senses. Stopped.

Heart. Halted.

Amazement. Elevated.

Because I hear the rest of his words before he speaks them.

Because my soul speaks the same ones.

"You're my one, Mishella Santelle." He pushes closer, tenderly compelling me to do the same. Dips his head until our noses slide close and our breaths tangle tight. "You're my bar of gold." His mouth, so beautiful and strong, brushes the parted wonder of mine. "And I'm hanging on with everything I've got."

"Cassian." It has no volume. Barely carries any air, for it really is not that either.

It is my prayer.

Of thanks.

Of worship.

Of love.

Of everything *I* am, deep in my most sacred being, opening for him. Flowering to him. Letting him into my body yet again, this time with the long, tender strokes that emulate the perfect twining of our souls...the forever commitment of our hearts. A joining that will take us into tomorrow—and whatever it brings—as well as all the tomorrows that come with it.

He is my gold.

No matter what.

CHAPTER SIX

CASSIAN

My fingers fly over the keyboard of my laptop, yanking amazed glances from the trio of housekeepers sitting at the next table over in the Palais Arcadia service staff lounge. I'm sure they're wondering who the hell let in the guy with the designer pants, boater shoes, and really wrinkled Henley, but after I toss over a wink and half a grin, they giggle. Now, I'm at least the *cute* lunatic at the next table over.

Back to business.

I finish up the fifty-third of ninety-three emails from yesterday. These are only the messages Rob, my assistant holding down the fort back at the office in New York, has deemed needing my attention as primary first responder right now. There are at least a hundred more in a second priority file, and double that in the "Only if You Have Time" folder.

If I'm lucky, I'll hit most of the first list before Ella wakes up.

Yes, I *do* remember that she ordered me to wake her sweet little ass up on the stroke of seven so she could be barging in on Samsyn by eight. I also remember the request getting interrupted by five yawns and two "what was I sayings" because of her jetlag—and that was before her nightmare.

Before I'd helped her get over it by getting my dick inside

her in any way I could.

Twice.

I shake my head, hoping the action dumps out the rest of the thoughts I need for this email—but after three tries, I still can't even spell the guy's name right. Maybe it's fate. Germans have complicated last names, so it's necessary to meet in person with them instead. I like Garrick too. Perhaps I can talk Ella into a quick side trip to Munich on the way back home...

My Instant Message window dings open—flaring with the colors she gleefully assigned to her pop-up window a few weeks ago. Pink and lavender as bright as a carousel horse frame one of her dopey-sweet grins—and a message of the opposite intent.

You were supposed to wake me up!

I laugh. Just a little. Only as much as she'd let me get away with, if she actually sat here fuming at me.

Not going to apologize for letting you rest—especially after what we did to sap your strength.

You mean what YOU did to fuck my head off?

My chuckle comes harder—though I can't summon the brass to correct her. Somehow, fucking her head off sounds a hell of a lot better than fucking her brains out—though after last night, I don't care if she calls it feeding the damn chickens. If she invites me upstairs to do it again, this laptop will be closed in three seconds, Rob's remaining forty emails be damned.

Another text buzzes in.

Getting dressed now. Where are you?

This, I seriously contemplate how to respond—then recognize, in light of all the bizarre twists this woman's life has taken since meeting me, that my answer won't raise even one of her eyebrows.

> *The palais service staff*
> *lounge. Handling some work.*

And enjoying the fact that it's not only the most peaceful space in the building but reminds me a lot of the employee cafeteria back at Court Towers. Hanging out at a little corner table there was first just my way to stay in touch with reality, remember where I came from—but after a while, it became one of the best getaways of my week. For big chunks of time, I'd found quiet and anonymity to actually get work done. When the nit-and-grit workers flowed in for their break periods, I had the chance to talk to them without filters or third parties. After a while, I wasn't even boss-man CEO to them anymore. I was just Cas, the eccentric guy with the loosened tie, chilling with his laptop at the corner table.

I miss those days. Am antsy to return to them soon—and now, bring Ella along too.

I want her to know every corner of my world. Fitting, since her love fills every corner of my heart.

I shall be right down.

Just like she ignites every inch of my grin. *Pegged it.* The woman responded so fast, it's clear she barely blinked, let alone rose a brow.

She's ready to go.

Which is why I hope Samsyn is too.

I ran into the guy earlier this morning—*much* earlier according to the Arcadian clocks, though my internal timer wasn't normal after Ella's nightmare got me up in more ways than one—and had a chance to express my woman's determination for a visit to Vylet Hester's place today. Syn had nodded tightly over his own cup of Tahreuse Mountain coffee, and said he'd work on making it happen. No time frame had been given, but pushing my luck before sunrise just hadn't seemed fair to the guy.

I text the man and am a little surprised when he responds by showing up in person. "Mishella bested you by two seconds," he explains, striding to the counter and pouring himself a cup of coffee. "And you are most correct. That little *tupalai* is on a tear to get to Vylet today."

Now the housekeepers rise and scatter, but not before gazing as if the Hulk himself has busted in and then splashed half a carton of creamer into his java. I don't know whether to send them off with a look of humor or commiseration. Although I can easily meet the man's gaze if we're chest-to-chest, Samsyn Cimarron is a daunting slab of a man, doing little to soften the image with his warrior's gait, piercing stare, and long dark hair. The shit's been hastily plaited off his face today, exposing his rugged features in sharper relief.

As he sits, the plastic chair beneath him squeaks in protest. "*Faisi-bana*," he mutters.

Smirk. "I prefer fucking my woman, but thanks for the offer."

He raises his head. Glares until his gaze is the color of a glacier. "I shall alert the media about that. Oh, wait." He cocks his head. "You and Mishella already told the whole damn *island* last night."

Screw the smirk. I flash a whole grin. "You looking for an apology?"

"Not particularly."

He releases a meaningful snort. I interpret the guy code at once. The midnight wake-up call wasn't good for just one couple in the prince's suite.

I chuckle while closing my laptop. "In that case, you're welcome."

The words are only seconds out of my mouth, and the laptop only halfway into its case, when a booming shout fills the little room.

"Cassian Cameron Jonathan Court. Put your hands up where we can see them. Now!"

"What the fu—"

"With all due respect, Prince Samsyn, you too."

Wisely, Syn complies. His hands and arms form a pair of upward right angles—though one breaks the pattern to toss aside a handgun mysteriously appearing from somewhere on him. Weirdly, I'm just as stunned by that as the onslaught of insanity that's hit the room, along with the four camouflage-covered soldiers following the lead of two black-suited men—if those ill-fitted things insist on being called suits.

Not the time to pull out your custom-fitted asshole, man.

Pseudo-baller one, with a haircut as government-issue as his threads, moves forward. His look might be shit, but his moves are well-practiced as he kicks Syn's gun toward the nearest soldier. Syn's vibration of a snarl stops the soldier in midgawk at the custom SIG, communicating one message alone. *Once you all are done with this BS, you* will *give that back.*

But what the hell is this BS?

The demand twists at my lips, nearly erupting as a growl of its own, especially as pseudo-baller two directs another soldier to grab my laptop. I direct the urge to better use, trying to place the guy's subtle accent. It's not Arcadian, though Samsyn's shock has already given me that detail. All at once, the connection clicks. *Dallas.*

The ballers are American.

Which makes the next detail click.

Bad suits. Worse haircuts. Brass baller attitudes.

They're CIA.

Goddammit, Damon.

MISHELLA

"Creator help me."

Somehow, past the thud of my heart in my throat, the words make it out. I am glad they are only a rasp, for the two soldiers in the hallway, training their guns and their attentions into the service lounge, have not heard a word. Their stress, so thick I can nearly see it in the air, flattens me against the wall of the stairwell I have just descended.

I peek at them in frantic glances. Who are they? What do they want? Are they connected to the bonsun who blew up the Grand Sancti Bridge? Is this the beginning of another part of their plot? Or maybe they are members of the extremist militant Pura, so devoted to extinguishing the Cimarrons and returning Arcadia to its extinct way of life, they tried taking over the palais from within just a few months ago.

And what if all of these monsters are interconnected?

Rune Kavill's ties to the Pura were believed severed after

their pathetic coup failed...

But if all of us have learned anything about Kavill, it is his likeness to a damn reptile—especially the gift of re-growing himself in all kinds of horrid ways.

"Now stand up slowly. I said *slowly*."

The directive comes from neither of the gunmen in the hallway. It booms from someone inside the lounge, *at* someone in the lounge.

Cassian.

I mold a terrified hand over my mouth, barely containing my scream. Breathe violently through my nose, forcing my fear to a manageable level—or I *think* I have, until compelling my quivering fingers across the keypad of my phone, into a text bubble directed at him.

WHERE ARE YOU?

A minute goes by.

No response.

Sounds come from inside the lounge. Scuffling feet. Steel against steel. Guns? Doing what?

Still no response.

Fear is all my blood is made of. The only thunder in my ears.

More clanking steel. Not guns.

Handcuffs?

"I'm sorry, sir. This is simply necessary." I do not recognize the voice, only to know it is gruff, American, and as "sorry" as a cop arresting the bad guy in a superhero movie—without realizing he is the good guy in disguise.

Suddenly, I miss superhero movies. And the big leather couch Cassian and I always watched them from at Temptation

Manor. And pigging on lemon bars and popcorn as we did. And the sounds of New York right outside the window.

And everything about the place I now realize as...

Home.

Just as much as all this.

Maybe even more...

A comprehension bearing the shittiest timing.

Especially as another voice answers Mr. Sorry-Not-Sorry.

"Tell that to someone who'll believe it, Agent Bullshit."

Cassian.

"Cassian!"

One of the soldiers whirls. The barrel of his gun swings out. If he fires, I'll likely lose my digestive system.

I do not care.

"Stop. Right. There!"

I do not listen.

"Dammit, I said *stop!*"

"Cassian!" My fear bursts to full throttle in it.

"Don't shoot her!"

But the thrust of *his* terror...

That stops me.

"What the hell is going on? Who the hell are you?" Like with all good onslaughts of fear, I explode into pure fury. Though I shake harder than before, I get both arms wrapped around myself. So much of me still does not care about their damn guns—but I must hold myself together, *somehow*, for Cassian. *Do not be afraid. Do not be afraid. Do not—*

I am nothing *but* fear. My very center feels split like a ripe pomegranate, my sanity turned into seeds, spilling everywhere...ready to be crushed underfoot.

And then they are.

Beginning the moment Cassian is led out into the hallway, his face grim, his arms bound by those awful cuffs...

"C-Cassian?" I battle not to throw myself at him. Even bind myself along with him. Instead I glare at the men grabbing him by both elbows. They wear faded black suits and smell like bagels and copier toner. I have not smelled copier toner in over two months, since my last few days of working in one of the office cubicles upstairs, but the alloy stench never leaves one's memory.

Just like I know this moment will never be completely erased either.

"What the bloody hell is going on?" I charge it at the man on the right. His eyes are a little kinder than his counterpart, who twists his lips as if his breakfast—actually a bagel, by the appearances of the crumbs on his lapels—has not agreed with him.

"It's Mishella, right?" he replies. "You're the girlfriend?"

"The betranli." I suck in a harsh breath, forcing the translation to mind. "I am his *fiancée* now."

"Shit." Bagel Suit snorts. "When did that happen, and why didn't we know about it?"

"None of your goddamn business." Cassian mutters it as if simply swapping one-liners with Doyle. If he thinks the bravado will fool me, he is wrong. He is standing here in real handcuffs, flanked by two men who clearly have the right to have rendered him that way. Thankfully, he seems to realize the same thing. In a calmer tone, he says to Kind Eyes, "Look. Leave her out of this, and I'll cooperate."

"Cooperate with *what*?" I do not want to snap it at him, but the expression is true—fear is the mother of anger—and right now, nothing but fear defines me.

Kind Eyes nods in the way used by doctors before breaking awful news to their patients. "I'm Agent Reyes and this is Agent McCree. We're with the US Central Intelligence Agency, permitted to be here by the Arcadian government."

"Fucking knew it," Cassian grumbles.

There is movement behind him. Lots of it. In stomping fury, Prince Samsyn appears. "You have permission," he barks, "but *not* authority. Especially not for this."

McCree shoots out a glare. "Even if we have cause to believe that the perpetrator of the Grand Sancti Bridge explosion was working for a contractor hired by Court Enterprises Incorporated?"

"Don't." Cassian cuts in before I can. His stare slashes into me with equal brutality. "Don't you goddamn *dare*, Ella." The curve of his lips becomes a tight line, but I hear his next words as if he utters them right into my mind. *Don't you dare tell them you already know this and we're helping Damon with it.*

With a furious huff, I lock my teeth and comply—but it is only because of love for him, not any shred of solidarity I might have developed for Damon. It has been *two days* since the bridge exploded. Certainly the CIA linked things backed to Cassian's company—but not enough to show up here and drag him off in handcuffs. They have more. Much more.

And only one person could have supplied them with all of it.

"Oh, she doesn't have to say a word, does she?" Bagel Man, now identified as Agent McCree, tacks on an assessing stare—at me. "That face *says* it all."

"Get your eyes off her goddamn face," Cassian snarls. "And everything else you're looking at."

McCree shrugs. "Cool your jets, Court. She's not my type."

"You going to tell me you used to get mistaken for a Hemsworth too?"

The man chuffs. "Nope. Just thinking the apple doesn't fall far from the tree. Selyna Santelle *is* one fine woman."

For the first time in the last five minutes, rage joins my fear. The only thing holding me back from acting on it is the confusion. Why the hell is this filthy *soldask* prattling about my *mother*—who may be a good many things but is smart enough to be those things *only* to my father. Affairs kill reputations faster than anything in this palais.

In my next breath, I realize I do not care. The man will lose his front teeth for it anyway. He is speaking about my *mother.*

But I wait one moment too long in deciding how to best deliver that fate.

The moment in which Cassian looks like he has been kicked in the gut.

"Fuck," he utters.

"What?" I blurt. "Cassian?" But when he yanks up his head, it is with an expression he lasers past me, down the hallway, as if he battles to burn a hole straight through the stone walls.

"Fuck," he repeats. "How did they...*why* would they..."

"They who?" I scurry around, planting myself in front of him—as if that stops Reyes and McCree from yanking him forward. I curl fists into Cassian's shirt, even as I'm forced to scramble backward. "They *who*?" I plead it again, begging for him to answer—because I don't want it to be what my gut is drives into me like a jammed nail gun. "Cassian! They who? *What* is going on?"

He stops so abruptly, I nearly topple to my backside. The agents jerk him, but he shirks them, a right shove and then a left, without tearing his stare from me.

His stare—which is suddenly green fire upon me.

Seizing me.

Sucking in the sight of me, as if the hallway is about to turn into a black hole and swallow me up.

"C-Cassian?"

And I thought I was already afraid.

I also thought fear was always cold. But now, all the ice in my veins is pure fire. My breath tastes like brimstone. My stomach is a mass of charcoal. My vision swims, truly threatening to turn the floor into a massive sanity suck. I sway from it, fighting back with blinks, trying to refocus back on Cassian...

To comprehend the words he desperately yells at me.

"Ella! Dammit. *Mishella!*"

"Wh-What?" A wisp, like smoke. *Pathetic. Speak up!* "What?"

Through some miracle, it gains enough volume. Cassian expels a breath filled with too much relief. Pulls it back in just as fast, hardening his features to tawny granite. "Listen. To. Me." After sending a come-at-me-again-and-pay-with-your-balls glare at Reyes and McCree, he whips back toward me. Dear Creator, even in his wrath, he is mesmerizing. "Find Doyle—"

"I can help with that." Samsyn issues the blistering growl, daring the agents with a glower to equal Cassian's.

"Thanks, Syn." Cassian acknowledges it in words but not movement. His stare, still a green firestorm, does not waver from me. "Go with him, Ella," he murmurs, pressing closer, summoning the very air around us in the way only he is capable of. At once, the molecules are spun into a bubble of exquisite perfection. How many times have I treasured that comparison, thinking nothing fit better than comparing our connection to the magic of spun color on the air?

Stupid, silly girl.

You picked bubbles?

Fragile.

Breakable.

Bubbles.

"*Ella.*"

"*What?*" It breaks through my tears, which I no longer try to hide. The damn man himself is smiling—*smiling!*—even when he knows I see straight through his act—that from the second McCree mentioned Mother and he reacted with that gape, I know their little "chat" yesterday was about much more than Maimanne and Paipanne's prenuptial arbitrations.

More importantly, what Cassian did not reveal to me about them.

So yes, dammit, he gets to see my tears. And know that they spring from being utterly enraged with him.

Utterly in love with him.

Stubborn, protective, determined, damnable, beautiful man.

"Go," he repeats softly. "Go *now*, with Samsyn." He clears his throat. "And find Doyle. And when you do, tell him he is ordered to take you back to New York. Immediately."

I push back. Then seize him harder. It is either that or slap him—which I may still resort to. "The fuck I will."

The fire in his gaze changes. Brightens. "You know I love it when you use that word with me, armeau, but—"

ANGEL PAYNE

Yes. Time to slap him. And I do.

At least it erases his smile. The resolution in his jaw is not any easier to stomach. "Mishella DaLysse—"

"Shut. Up." I grab him again, this time roping my arms around his neck. Drag his head down, forcing him to kiss me fiercely. "I will *not* do it. Dammit, Cassian. I will not!"

"You *will*." He parts his lips, exposing his locked teeth. "This isn't just a firm request, my love. I'm giving you an order."

"No." I pull him close on a brutal sob. "*No.*"

"I'll be okay." He pushes the words into my mouth. "*We'll* be okay. But you must get out of here, right now."

"Why?" I implore it with all the intensity in my body. "*Why?*"

"Because..." He stops himself, darting a pair of alert glances back at both his captors. "If things have gone cocked-up like I think they have, I don't want you to be your parents' next prey."

"Dammit." The syllables, broken and furious, burn their way up my throat. "I *knew* it."

His jaw tightens more. His stare takes on its jade dagger hue. "Do *not* speak to them, Ella. Do you hear me? You find Doyle, get on the fucking plane, and let him take your ass back to Temptation, where you'll be safe."

He drives in the dictate with a hard, demanding kiss. In the thrust of his tongue and the hunger of his mouth, I feel every drop of his fervent desire—and his consuming fear.

We do not pull apart until McCree and Reyes force, yanking him back with mutterings about getting a room and how they don't want to start tipping us for the show. But Cassian fights them—now, I know, for the last time—to bore one last stare into me, sweeping his command through every last corner of me...

Before whispering guttural words to me.

"You are my bar of gold, Ella Santelle."

I fight to answer him, but words clog my throat, bound by the ache in my heart. By the time my body feeds me enough strength to get them out, he is pulled away, his face still shining with the sheen of *my* tears.

"And you are the best contract I ever signed, Cassian Court."

CHAPTER SEVEN

CASSIAN

Karma is sometimes a raving lunatic bitch.

I glare at the stone block walls and archaic architectural amenities of my "cozy" little waiting room somewhere in Censhyr Prison and force myself not to flip a middle finger at the harpy. I can practically hear her rolling in the glee, replaying how I pulled up images of this place for Fortin and Selyna yesterday.

Or maybe the dynamic duo has had their own gloating laughter piped into my head.

In which case, I'll not give them the benefit of even one middle finger.

I rise from the steel table, letting my "designer" aluminum chair clatter to the floor, glad at least the handcuffs are removed now. That was eight hours ago.

Interesting...all the things a guy can get straight in his head after eight hours.

Like exactly how hungry he has to be for *grawl*.

I contemplate the point while perusing the two bowls I left behind on the table. One is empty, the other still more than half-full of the Arcadian "specialty," a porridge-meets-poi sort of thing. Even with my rumbling gut, I can barely look at the shit now. At least the cut fresh fruit in the other bowl was plentiful and juicy. Guess I don't have to worry about scurvy today.

I'd laugh at my own joke, if I wasn't so busy pacing.

And battling the echoes of laughter in my head, now my only company. A guy takes what he can get in a ten-by-ten cubicle formed from hundred-year-old granite blocks.

Even the chuckles of the two people who have flipped the bitch on him.

And *there's* my friend karma again.

I'm only two laps into my pacing therapy when one of the room's two doors opens. It's not the one through which McCree brought me in—apparently, Reyes got stuck with filling out the paperwork—so I expect a prison guard or some "appropriate" lawyer-type person to appear.

I halt, my shock likely apparent, to see Samsyn Cimarron's dark head barely clear the antiquated archway.

"Hi, honey. I have arrived in the home."

Spurted laugh. Whether it's the irony of the setting or the absurdity of how the guy just butchered that, I have no idea. "Tell Brooke she needs to have you work on that one a little more—but I'm grateful for the break, especially after the *grawl*."

Samsyn's lips twist in sympathy. He holds up a steel cup. "That is why I brought you this."

The water, tasting a lot like the alloy in which it's contained, is still better than the beige paste still lining my mouth. I gulp the shit down and then shake my head at the cup. "I'll never complain about all the steel in Manhattan again."

Syn's grimace deepens. "On that note..."

And torques the scowl on mine too. "What?" I snap.

A grunt escapes him. "Whatever it is these bonsuns think

they have on you...they think it is fairly strong." He braces both hands to the back of the still-upright chair in the room. "I went in to ask them if they would release you into my custody. Promised them I would keep you in my suite at the palais, with round-the-clock guards." His shoulders tighten beneath the bulky black jacket of his uniform. "They told me that they respected me too much to put me in that situation."

"That situation...of what?"

"Harboring a terrorist."

I pivot away. Try focusing on the crevices in the concrete walls, even counting the seams between the bricks, to bring down the spike in my fury.

It feels a hell of a lot better to hurl the goddamn cup.

"Cassian—"

"It's bullshit." I twist my head back around. "You know that, Syn—right?"

Immediate nod—though questions linger in his piercing eyes. "Cassian..."

I take two hard, deliberate steps. They bring me full face with him again. "It's all right," I assert. "Ask me. Go ahead."

Obeying warrior's code, the man honors me by rising to his full height. "What *do* they have on you?"

"Plenty," I respond right away, "if I assume Selyna and Fortin Santelle did what I think they did."

"*Dégan kimfuks.*" As the oath spills, his lips snarl up. "Why does that shock me as little as an Eve District whore?"

I give him the courtesy of a dark chuff. "Well, don't high-and-mighty it all yet. I'm as much to blame."

His thick brows bunch. "Huh?"

"I loaded the damn gun and then handed it to them."

"The fuck?"

"Remember how I pulled them out of the room yesterday? After you and I spoke out on the terrace?"

"Of course." He nods. "Because you wanted to be honorable about your marriage proposal to Mishella." Then snorts. "As if that pair would know 'honorable' if it bit them on the asses."

"Yeah, well..." I take a deep breath. "The honorable shit was the easy part." Start to pace again, though not with the intent of Thor-hammering a new pathway into the concrete anymore. As crazy as it sounds, just getting to talk about it lightens the bricks in my gut. Christ. *Could Kate have been right all these years?* My college friend, Kate Robbe, has preached to me for years about the value of feeling better about even life's worst by simply talking through it. Guess I owe her a bottle of her favorite Cabernet when I get back to real life.

If I get back to real life.

"What do you mean, the easy part?"

Syn's prompt brings me back to the subject. "Naturally, they brought up a prenup."

"Naturally." He shakes his head, looking near disgusted.

I square my stance. "For the record, I'd give every cent in my bank account to Mishella."

"For the record, I believe you." But across his face is the rest of his truth: that he'll always remember how I got Ella's attention in the first place.

I borrow boardroom tactics to deal with that tidbit. *Don't dwell on what can't be reversed.*

Especially, dear Christ, because I must focus now what *can* be. Of what has to happen.

Convincing him of what *really* happened.

"I went into that meeting with them yesterday knowing

they knew it as well." Another corporate tactic comes to my aid. Clasping hands at my back helps steel my resolve when confessing the rest. "But I had an ace in *my* pocket." I meet his stare head on, knowing he won't respect it any other way. "There was proprietary information to Court Enterprise's selection process for each of the Arcadian infrastructure contracts—things only insiders would have known and then passed along to the companies bidding on the jobs."

For the first time since I've known the man, I see what real shock looks like on his face. Does nothing to turn his dark wolf into a puppy. "Are you saying..."

"That Fortin and Selyna knew all of those things?" In one motion, I scoop up my fallen chair and then slide into it. Bad move. I instantly yearn to pace again but force myself to stay put, projecting taut control. "Yeah. That's exactly what I'm saying."

One chair up, one chair down. Syn hurls the one he's been massaging in favor of slamming both fists to the table and leaning forward. "So *they* were the ones who potentially exposed this country's infrastructure to Rune Kavill's fuckery?" He answers his own question before I can, its fury twisting down his massive arms and into those fists again. "By the Creator's filthy balls, why?" He pushes up, circling the space behind him with vicious stomps. "Fuck. Do not answer that. I know why."

Weirdly—maybe not so—watching him fume brings me a new infusion of calm. "Yeah, well...*I* should've known why." I trace a figure eight on the table with my middle finger. "But I thought, after how those two jumped at signing our first contract, they'd readily choose luxury over responsibility."

"You mean money over power?" His grunt is drenched

in derision. "Snowball's chance in hell, my *arkami*. They sold Mishella off to you because of those infrastructure contracts you dangled along with the agreement—and because they waited so long for the perfect match for her at court, most of those 'potential husbands' were nonexistent." He picks up his toppled chair and then straddles it backward. "What did you offer with the new contract?"

I draw my hand back—and resist the urge to snap every one of the fingers in it. It's the hand responsible for inking that damn contract—and setting this insane set of events into motion. "Wasn't what I offered," I mutter. "It was what I demanded in return."

Samsyn's head rocks back. Comprehension washes his face. "Because you suspected..."

"They were in league with Kavill."

"*Dammit.*" His head falls forward. Shakes slowly. "I would have suspected the same shit pile, given that trail to go on."

I lean back. Brace elbows on the arms of the chair. "So I told them that if they took the money, they'd immediately forfeit all positions directly or indirectly affecting Arcadian governmental policy."

His gaze narrows. "Including Fortin's seat on the High Council?"

I arch a brow. "If I was ready to toss those two a bone, *that* wouldn't be the one."

"You do not seem like the bone-throwing type."

Despite the combination of grunt and laugh turning it into a compliment, my chest is still a meat grinder of regret—and stress. "Yeah, well—they went ahead and took the fucking thing for themselves."

"By biting off the hand it came on at the same time."

I abhor the tight nod of agreement I have to give up. "I gave too much fucking slack in their leashes. Clearly, they found a way to convince the CIA that I was colluding with Kavill and bribing them to keep quiet about it."

"In other words..." He turns the hand over, fingers spread. "Complete fiction?"

My jaw clenches harder. Tooth enamel is overrated—but possessing a long memory isn't. The hitch in his question, so subtle it's nearly negligible, hooks me right back to the fact that he and Evrest weren't even prepared to let us land the plane yesterday morning. *We can go right back there if you want, man.*

It's a commitment worth standing for. "*You* give *me* the answer to that, Cimarron," I challenge while doing so. "By now, your people have seen every file I have about those contractors. I walked right into this palais with that laptop—"

I'm cut off, understandably so, as he suddenly lurches up. Growls with low meaning, "That...laptop..."

"That I gave you full access to." Maybe he needs a not-so-graceful reminder? "That your IT team cloned nearly half the files on, using their magic little stick—"

"The...laptop..."

I start sliding around the table. Is the big guy having a stroke or some shit, in the middle of my holding room? I glance up at the monitoring cameras—ancient pieces of crap; wouldn't be surprised if they're in place simply for show these days—and wonder who the hell will hear me through these cinder blocks if the mountain of a man goes down on me...

"The *laptop.*"

"Cimarron?" The demand feels justified, as he looks up with a probing glare. "You feeling all right?"

"No." His retort is immediate but distant.

"Because of the laptop?"

"That sat on the damn table in the sitting room yesterday," he fills in. "While Brooke and Mishella 'chatted' on the chaise, and you and I 'escaped' out to the terrace..."

"Meaning the thing wasn't attended or watched for a good twenty minutes," I fill in.

"Meaning Fortin and Selyna had plenty of time to jab in a few memory sticks of their own."

I frown. There's logic to his thinking...but not. "But that was before I met with them...even brought up the new agreement. Why would they think—"

"That a man who built a worldwide engineering empire in under five years would not eventually discover their connection to Kavill?" He starts to pound out that circle in the floor again, only to stop and cock a questioning look back. "How *did* you put it all together so swiftly?" When my first response must resemble something between conflict and fury, he presses, "What? You could tell me, but then you would have to kill me?"

I try to laugh, even bitterly. "You need a firm yes or no on that?"

Three seconds, maybe four, pass for him to process that— before my words act like beats in a fucking Bond movie and the second door to the room opens. Striding through the portal are two figures, so elegantly suited-out I don't recognize them at first.

Once I do, I want to fall back into my chair.

Or pick the damn thing up and use it on them.

Yeah. *Both* of them.

"What the fucking hell are you doing here?"

Slam of a briefcase. Hint of a grim smile. "Nice to see you

again too, little brother."

I narrow a glare. "Why did you suck face with a tarantula?"

"What?"

"Then let it camp out on top of your head?"

Damon whacks the side of my head. "If I had, you'd still thank me for it, douche bag." He gloats for a second, observing I'm too shocked to fight back physically *or* verbally. "In case you can't tell, I'm in disguise."

"Oh, I can tell." I jerk the top of my head toward the camera. "But now they can too."

"No, they can't." Doyle, also sporting extra "tarantula" on his face and a wig only slightly better than Damon's, adds, "Only the video works on those things."

Samsyn nods. "The audio has been out for years." Then grunts my direction. "We were planning on letting Court Enterprises bid on upgrades."

It comes as a bigger relief than I expected—only because I hate that they're both here. At least now I can find out why.

"So...what? Are you supposed to be my 'lawyers' or something?"

Doyle slides his briefcase next to Damon's and pops the latches. "They call them *juristes* here, but yeah. And while we're at it, you're welcome. I'm going to get that out of the way right now."

"That so?" I fold my arms, focusing on keeping the chaos in my brain from blowing the top of my skull off. This really is feeling more and more like a Bond movie—only it's one of the strange ones with the weirder-than-weird plot twists, instead of a Daniel Craig classic. "And I'm thanking you for...what, exactly?"

Doyle chucks an irked glare. Shrugs like I've just asked if

my nose is still in the middle of my face. "Breaking you out of here."

Now I do laugh. And really wonder if I *am* in a movie—in which this pair, with testicles big enough for Shaquille O'Neal's autograph, have really declared their intention to bust me out of Censhyr Prison with the island's security forces leader standing five feet away.

Especially when I glance to Samsyn, brows raised in a clear plea for commiseration, and he answers with a neutral, nearly scary, nod. "Anything I can do to help?"

I go ahead and fall into my chair. "You three have shitty timing for this, you know."

"Our timing's perfect." Damon's tightened cheek displays the scar from when I backhanded him with a Megatron figure at my eleventh birthday party. "The guards switch shifts in ten minutes, so they won't be paying as much attention."

"Fuckhead," I mutter. "I mean this episode of one of those prank-the-putz TV shows. That's what this is, right?" I throw another stare at Syn. "You didn't really just ask them if you could *help* with this insanity, right?"

The guy scowls. "What is a *putz*?"

Doyle snickers.

"Dammit," I mutter.

"You want out of here or not?" Damon demands.

"And yes, I will help," Samsyn reiterates—while warning me off with a pointed finger. "Look. I had nothing to do with what those two kimfuks pulled this morning or all the bullshit that has happened since. Only two things are stopping me from opening this place's front gate and pushing you out myself."

I narrow my glare. "Make a joke about your balls, and I'll spill about what Brooke likes calling you in bed."

The big guy almost looks ready to deck me for that but bypasses it to continue, "One, your country is owed our respect, despite stomping into my sandbox without permission this morning. Two, I would rather not have to face a mountain of crap from my woman *and* my king." His stare turns to ice once more. "But if this is how the CIA usually plays—"

"It isn't." Damon steps forward, squaring shoulders in respect to Syn. "Not usually, at least." He exhales hard. "But if they're shitting over so much of your sandbox, it means they're being pressured—big-time—to get this bad guy notched on the bedpost. And"—as he looks my way, his gaze perceptibly darkens—"they've got enough evidence to do it."

I continue looking back at him through sheer force of will, stuffing away every last thing I'm really feeling. Thank fuck I've logged so many years of doing this with corporate adversaries, it's almost natural. Damon is far from an adversary—but no way in hell is he friend either. Not yet.

Perhaps not ever again.

Samsyn firms his stance once more. Cocks his head. "And you know all of this about the CIA...why?"

I curl a knowing sneer. "Prince Samsyn, meet my brother, Damon Court, aka Bourne Jackson, with the United States Central Intelligence Agency."

Syn gives us a good three seconds to view his jacked eyebrows. "Bourne....Jackson? As in Jason and Samuel? Clever—and kick-ass."

Damon's grin is ear-to-ear. "I like him."

"Are we getting to a point here?" I look at Samsyn but stab my head toward Damon. "We know all of this because he's one of those fuckers."

Damon's smile is still eerily lazy.

"*Was* one of them."

And *that* would be the reason.

Which doesn't feel as vindicating as it should.

"Ah. *That's* why you tongued out the tarantula."

That is vindicating.

Until he turns, glaring. Wearing an expression I haven't seen since I relentlessly ribbed him about locking braces with Cynthia Sabala in sixth grade. "To get in here and save *your* sorry ass, you mean?"

And like then, I also hear the hurt beneath his wrath.

Unlike then, I'm not too full of myself to reach out and clamp his shoulder.

Also unlike then, I vow not to take a second of being with him for granted. I may still be pissed and confused about why he helped the CIA fake his own death and then hide it from Mom and me for over ten years, but I'm not so stupid to think he won't disappear again. But hearing that he's dropped the assholes is already a giant salve on that wound. Or have *they* dropped *him*? And does it really matter?

"All right." It's also my version of *I'm sorry*. I only hope he still gets me enough to know that. "What happened?"

He takes half a second to acknowledge my contrition with a jab of his jaw—thank fuck—before growling, "I took all the information to the office. *Not* the New York branch. I flew it all straight down to headquarters, in Langley—"

"All the shit from the bulletin boards?" *A lot* of information I'd never been meant to see, thanks to a streak of jealousy about Mishella Santelle I wouldn't—and won't ever—apologize for. It had led to me tracking her down at the hotel where she and Damon had been working together for almost two weeks, searching for precise details linking Rune Kavill's phony engineering and architectural firms to at least two-thirds of my Arcadian infrastructure contractor list.

Translation: Anyone with their hands on that list could easily infer I'd known all about it first.

A fact that couldn't be further from the truth.

The only reason *I'd* learned of it was because of barging in on him and Ella—literally—in that suite at the Marquis, where those bulletin boards dominated the room like a damn murder investigation, carefully tracking down the *wheres, whys,* and *hows* of Kavill's massive deception.

The seeds of his plans to ruin Arcadia, one disaster at a time.

"Yeah." Damon's response to my surmise is clipped—but hedges at more. *A lot* more. "But by the time I got into the office, the international witch hunt had started." He glances pointedly at Samsyn. "The Arcadians are the new darlings of the international business world. Everyone looks at this place as their new little pet, ready to be dressed up and played with—"

"We are no one's *little* anything. Nor do we play fucking dress-up."

"Heard and acknowledged." Damon nods. "Loud and clear. But you're talking about the CIA, Your Highness—and in the case of a high-profile manhunt like this, they'll 'ask' for your cooperation only for the sake of protocol." His face discernibly tightens. "Believe me, they already assume they have it."

I toss in a reluctant nod. "He's right, Syn. And you're not in a place to turn them down, even politely."

A violent rumble emanates from the prince's gut. I don't want to be gratified by Syn's struggle, but...

Who the fuck am I kidding? It feels *great*.

"Welcome to international politics, Highness." Doyle adds it with that "special" certainty of his, hinting at a past he's never told me about—or likely will. "When the world's largest secret spy agency offers to jump in 'help,' the only correct answer is 'thank you, and what do you need from us?'"

Samsyn's thick brows practically collide above his nose. "Like my boot up their ass, per se?"

Diffusion has become a necessity.

If the table was an oak oval and a view of Manhattan stretched at my feet instead of a concrete slab, I'd order Syn to take a coffee break and come back. Not a choice here. I go for option two. Lift my gaze to my brother and query, "So what finally happened? At the agency?"

Damon's face hardens. *Here's* an expression I've never viewed on him before—and goddammit, it's daunting. "Nothing."

"Nothing?" I spread my arms. "Well, D, clearly it was *something*." I haven't dragged myself to the Arcadian version of the tundra for the sake of curiosity.

He grimaces. "Shit. Mom's let you turn into a cheeky little tyke, hasn't she?"

"News flash. I haven't been a 'tyke' since the day you died."

"Huh?" Syn injects.

"*There's* a meme waiting to happen," Doyle murmurs.

My glare yanks Damon back to the summary. "I meant nothing happened that they'd let *me* see."

"But it was your investigation."

"Sure as hell seemed that way, didn't it?" He jams both hands into his pockets. "Until it suddenly...wasn't." His lips press tighter. "Those fuckers just took everything I had, thanked me for my service, and told me to go home until I was called up for my next assignment."

"Fuckers," Samsyn mutters.

"About what I said," Damon returns. "But officially, they own everything down to the Calvins on your cock from the moment you walk through their big shiny doors."

Samsyn rises up. Writhes through a movement strangely close to a shudder. "What are 'Calvins'?"

Doyle snorts. "Too little fabric for too much money."

I credit him for the humor with a matching sound and little else. Doesn't seem right when my brother still looks prepared for a tornado to hit the room. "They came for my satchel," he relays. "And I almost didn't give it to them. Something didn't feel right."

"But you *did* give it to them."

Samsyn's tone is dark but oddly non-accusing. Damon, bracing both hands to the table, looks up like a guy directly in the path of his dreaded twister. "I had no choice."

"No," Syn replies. "You did not." He responds as a fellow warrior, a man who understands the bonds that form with people who have kept one's secrets. He doesn't know even the half of that depth between my brother and the CIA.

Which makes the desolation on Damon's face rip into me even harder.

And the fury in his voice like a goddamn razor on the air.

"I almost knew, then and there, what they were going to do with all of it." He drops his gaze to me. "That every word I said about your innocence was just noise to them. That somehow, *you* were going to end up being the Bin Laden for that bridge disaster."

"Though nothing could be further from the truth." Doyle's

accusation is an equally savage gash. "All Cassian's wanted to do was help this fucking place." He finishes with an apologetic shrug to Samsyn. Syn shrugs back. Two peas of similar temper recognize their mutual pod.

But my bury-it-until-it-kills-me brother drops his head into his hands.

"Shit." He digs hands into his hair, drags them backward, and then clutches them together in back. I stare at his twisted fingers, wondering why my mind can't connect them...to *him*. Why, in so many ways, the man he's become seems a different person than the boy I grew up with.

Perhaps because...he is. Maybe it's really just that simple. And painful.

"I knew what they were going to do," he finally utters. "I knew it, in my gut, before everything else confirmed it. Just sensed they'd somehow gotten additional evidence and were going to use it to fuck you like this." He lifts his face, aged ten years in the last five minutes—*not* helped by the fuzzy fake hair—and gores me with a nearly black gaze. "I knew it, Cas, and it made me sick to my stomach. You have to believe me."

Part of me is wrung deeper from his desolation. Another part, smaller but giving similar orders, craves more.

Enough to make up for fourteen years of having to live without him.

"Hell."

I mumble it, disconcerted. Yearn to be disconnected too. Wanting to feel anything but what I do right now. Hell...longing to feel *nothing*. But that's not the case. That's not the truth. That's not the fact that he's here in disguise instead of with his "buddies" Reyes and McCree, meaning he's probably gone rogue on the CIA for me. Given all of it up for me. Literally come back from the dead for me.

The truth is...

this.

The stare we share, stripping the years away and bringing brotherhood back.

The embrace we surge into, sealing that commitment. Fading that loss with new love.

Emotion is a brutal assault, pounding sharp stings behind my eyes—forcing me to yank back before it turns to full-on sap.

"I believe you, motherfucker." I confirm the point as any good little brother would: by ramming his shoulder nearly hard enough to dislocate it. But I don't—because I know how far I can push it with him. Because I always will.

And the surety of it fills me.

And makes me grin like an idiot, despite everything that's so wrong about this damn mess.

And makes Damon smirk back. "Glad we got that settled, douche bag." The sheen in his own eyes is blinked back after its two-second cameo. "Now let's focus on the important part of all this."

"About goddamn time." Doyle shifts forward and swivels his briefcase around so the lid blocks the direct angle of the camera's lens. He shuffles the piles of papers inside, which turn out to be a disguise of their own. The compartment actually contains a dress shirt, tie, and suit jacket.

My shirt, tie, and jacket.

I contain my features into a baseline of composure, though I don't have to be so careful about my switchblade of a growl. "What the fuck?"

Damon speaks to Doyle as if they're conferring *juristes*— and sure as hell not like I'm sitting there next to him. "I don't think we'll need the shirt. They didn't make him change clothes or anything—"

"Because they haven't actually arrested me?" I break in.

"Good point."

Again as if I'm not even here.

"So we skip the shirt—"

"Makes things faster."

"He can just cinch the tie around his neck." Doyle tosses the tie my general direction. "Then wear the jacket on top."

Damon smirks. "Too bad we can't take a picture for posterity. I bet every fashion blog in New York would actually think Henleys and ties has become a new thing."

Doyle lobs back a chuckle. "You have no idea."

"Regrettably, I do. You know what it's like to walk through the airport and see your little brother on the cover of every gossip rag, telling off the glam-girl news babe on national TV?"

"Sitting right here," I interject in a growl.

"Well, that must've been surreal." Out of the briefcase comes something resembling another tarantula on the loose, slid my way beneath a sheaf of "legal papers" this time. I don't pick it *or* the tie up.

"Once more, sitting *right* here, assholes."

"A situation we're working to resolve, *asshole*." Damon turns, bringing a fresh glare with him—resulting in *my* new urge to smack it off his chiseled face. With this new chance to look at him and actually process the fact, I realize a lot has changed about his face—creases, tension, even a jagged scar over his left eye—but so much hasn't changed. The dimples that match mine. The slight bump in his nose from where he endo'ed off his bike and broke it. The cocky sonofabitch who still lives at the back of his dark-green gaze. Yeah, especially that. Thus the craving to lay him out.

But like the Court kid who actually *listened* to Mom, I decide to use my words instead. "The situation is what it is, D. And it won't be 'resolved' like this."

He clutches into stillness—creating room for Doyle's hissed profanity. This much I've expected—though Samsyn's grunt is a weird cherry on the stunned guys' sundae.

"Excuse the fuck out of me?" Damon finally grits.

I jerk back to my feet. "You heard me."

Doyle rolls out one of his slow, classic snarls. "*Cas.*"

"What?"

"Now isn't the time to play Gallahad."

"Not playing a thing." I wheel back around. Once again, instinct dictates my take-charge boardroom stance. "What kind of a message does an escape send?" Though the answer creeps across all their faces, I voice it. "As fabricated and twisted as their information is, an escape instantly paints me in guilt. And we all know light shades lead to darker ones—before they become permanent ink."

"God*dam*mit." Damon drops his fist so hard, everything on the table jumps. "This is the CIA, dumb shit—working a high-profile incident. Shades of *anything* don't come into play here, nor do right, wrong, truth, or the facts. These bastards just need someone in the general vicinity of 'most likely.' A sap they can turn into an example on the guillotine, in order to appease the pissed-off mobs." He storms to his feet. "And guess whose pretty gold head they're targeting for that, brother?"

He keeps coming at me, stopping just a breath away. I let him seethe, knowing I'm about to make his torment worse—but refusing to sugarcoat my truth for him.

"*I* don't run from my fights, Damon."

Rage blasts through his eyes. Fuels the indignation across his face...swiftly dissolving into resignation and then shame. And remorse.

It's a shit fest to watch. So many emotions I could wipe free—by just combing my hair, cinching a Windsor around my neck, and then letting him and Doyle lead me out of here. With Samsyn's *blessing*.

But it's not the right thing.

No matter what the fuck they think.

"Okay, knock that the hell off." Unfortunately, Doyle already has my number about this. Has had it since the day I hired him, for reasons I can't or don't want to fathom—but right now, am damn irked by. "He's right, you idiot. You need to stop living in another galaxy and get the hell over yourself, Obi-Wan."

"Excuse me?" Damon and I retort it together.

Doyle rolls his eyes. "This light saber is going to slice you in two, yeah? But you're not a fucking Jedi, Cas. You don't get to come back as a floating head or a fun little voice in anyone's ear." He plunges a finger to the table. "This is the Death Star, and you need to shove the hell off."

It's effective. I'll give him that much. Even more now than after D's guillotine speech, I battle to clearly listen to the whisper of the Force in my own head. I'm stunned when only silence responds—before realizing that for some reason, that voice has always sounded like Damon. But now, he's no longer my guiding ghost of right. He's my reality of confusion. And Doyle, who's always, *always* had my back, is poised there in a matching cheapo wig and glare of conviction.

"Asshole," I mutter at him from locked teeth. "I should've ordered Ella to take you back on the plane with her."

Once more, he goes completely still.

This time, turning me into an ice sculpture with him.

Especially when he growls, "What are you talking about?"

I force my body to move. To step toward him, every step a match to the cannonball thuds of my heart. "Mishella," I utter. "She found you, right? I told her—*ordered her*—to find you and coordinate with Laith and the plane so she could—"

Screw it.

His face, suffused with a mix of *holy shit* and *dammit to hell*, silences the rest of it in me.

Then turns it all into agony.

"Cas—"

"Save it." I look up, making it clear I want my next answer with no fuss, no remorse, and complete honesty. "Just tell me... *did* she even *find* you?"

His mouth flattens, causing the mustache to writhe like a dying caterpillar. *Not amusing*—because I'm pretty damn sure what he's about to confess.

"She secured the disguises for us."

Damon leans over. "And supplied detailed instructions for back roads in and out of here."

I glare over my shoulder at Samsyn. He raises both hands, stretching the black uniform across his Montana mountain range of a chest, while protesting, "It is all fresh fuckery to me, arkami. I got her to Doyle and then ran off to the six alerts screaming for my attention."

I look back to the Double D's of steel-plated *cojones*. Grip the edge of the table, watching my fingers go white as I resist the urge to completely flip it over—instead shoving it back by a foot, as a new sensation winds into the feeling. Something tainting my rage. Weakening it.

No.

Changing it.

Forcing it into the hugest sensation I've fought since McCree and Reyes first clamped me into handcuffs.

Fear.

Not garden-variety dread. Not even a giant fist in the gut.

This is shit I've never experienced before, threatening to combust me from the inside out—and it gets worse as I imagine Ella somewhere on this island, thinking she's actually going to justify her disobedience by telling me it "all worked out" because she helped Doyle and Damon break me out of Censhyr Prison.

The little scammer couldn't be more wrong.

And if fate will give me one goddamn break today, letting me reach the woman before her scheming parents, she's going to learn exactly *how* wrong.

I snatch up the tie, throw it around my neck, and loop the fastest Windsor knot I'm capable of. Doesn't detract me from firing a determined nod at Doyle and then my brother.

"Tell me what the plan is, and then let's get the fuck out of here."

MISHELLA

I'd forgotten how vast the sky truly is. And how many stars it can really hold.

I let my head rock back, overwhelmed by the blanket of silver-spun light over my head. Even here, with the torchieres along the palais balconies still lit, there is but a fraction of the light noise generated by the machine known to this solar system—and perhaps several more—as Greater Manhattan.

Part of me misses the constant energy and movement and life of the city: the beeps, honks, shouts, sirens, and constancy of my second home. A bigger part misses the actual place that makes it such. I wonder how things are faring at Temptation Manor at this moment. Is Hodge puttering with something or seeing to the landscaping? Has Prim baked a treat for him to enjoy when he is finished? Is Scott down in the garage, tending to one of Cassian's cars, or perhaps in his little office, studying for a test at university?

I miss it.

I really do.

But it will *never* be home without Cassian.

And it will never give me back the stars.

I wince. This is a good cautionary lesson for a mental journal. *Do not crowd Cassian and the stars onto adjoining thoughts—at least not while they are free and he is not.*

Fat lot of good it does for my next morbid musing.

"Can you see the stars too, my love?" My whisper mixes with the soft ocean breeze. It smells amazing, like jasmine and sea brine, but I hardly notice. "Are you looking at the sky and even thinking of me, my *donné raismette*?"

My man. My reason.

I lift a clenched hand to the empty hole in my center. There is movement there, the steady thud of an organ with its valves and ventricles and arteries and veins, but there is no life. Not *my* life. A torment that just got worse throughout this horrific day...begun with watching those CIA bonsuns drag him away in handcuffs...

Nearly ten hours later, nothing has been made clearer. Not a shred of news has come forth from Censhyr. I struggle to keep my wits and my sanity, even to let Vylet speak inside my mind despite her refusals to do so to my face. *No news is good news, wench.*

The words just crash and burn in my heart.

"No news in *what* damn way?" I mutter to myself. "You mean, no news like they have not thrown him completely in prison yet...or no news like they are simply preparing to do it in the US instead of here? And does it make any damn difference, anyway?"

"At this point? Nope."

The day has been so surreal, I wonder if the night is simply following suit by giving new voices to my internal conversations—until Brooke steps outside with me. She brings an added, small token in the form of instant curiosity.

Make that a big bite of *what the hell.*

I was prepared to simply ask why she dimmed all the lights in her wake. My second query takes immediate precedence.

"Has 'girl ninja' become a new fashion statement at court since I left?"

She follows my stare down her form. She is clad in a padded black jacket and matching combat pants, tucked into mud-encrusted boots—contrasted by the sudden blaze of her grin, showing up well beneath the purposeful black smudges on her face. Though her blond curls are tamed into a severe bun, I am certain the black fabric bunched around her neck is actually a form-fitting hood, used to conceal those strands under different circumstances.

"Not when I last checked," she drawls, answering my question. "But when have you known me to check?"

I cock my head. Crunch up my nose. Murmur warningly, "Brooke..."

"Hmm?"

"What have you been up to?" Folded arms. Suspicious stare. "And why?"

She leans on the rail, crossing one ankle over the other. "Not nearly as interesting a story as what *you're* about to be up to."

Like a picture suddenly coming into focus, cognizance fully hits—spilling my gasp. "By the Creator."

"Hmmm. He helped a little. I suppose."

"Brooke!"

If Vy were here, jibes would be flying about the decibel damage of my squeal and whether I was breaking a princess of Arcadia with my hug. But only Brooke's laugh fills my ears as she hugs back just as fiercely.

"Does this mean, maybe once, you'll forgive the dirt under my fingernails?"

"Crazy tupalai." I tease it back through tears. "For this, I may never look beneath your nails again."

"Yessss." She fist-bumps the air and then steps back with mock contrition. "I need to be honest. I only helped after the hard part was done. Doyle and Damon risked much more."

I follow the jerk of her head, sobbing as the two men come into view, followed by Samsyn. I rush over but do not maul them as I did Brooke; if they are injured, I do not want to damage them more. But both curl up grins reminding me of swaggering dogs, despite the strange black stains over their eyes. No. Not stains. Stepping closer, I recognize they have each torn their "mustache" in two, then plastered the pieces back on as eyebrows.

Damon wiggles his before declaring, "The tarantulas have landed. We repeat: the tarantulas have landed."

"*All* of them?" I shake while forcing myself to ask it.

Doyle's smile mellows—just a little. He finally murmurs, "Yeah. *All* of us."

Joyous sob. Uncontrollable. Bursting free. "It *worked*? He just walked out with you?"

Doyle nods and chuckles. "To be fair, Samsyn helped."

My prince smirks. "Fake fighting is even more enjoyable than the real thing."

"Dammit," Brooke mutters. "I still missed all the fun."

"Psssh," Doyle snorts. "He had to lose, you know. He was the distraction."

Brooke quirks a saucy brow. "When my man loses, you *bet* it's a distraction."

"Yes, well." Syn shrugs. "Sometimes the ballsiest moves are the best ones."

Damon starts to laugh as well but cuts himself short. "It was *all* pretty freaking ballsy."

"Aw, c'mon." Doyle drags it out, scoffing. "You've surely pulled off ballsier shit."

Damon's snort is noncommittal. "Maybe. but I had bigger crowds to work with than a few overworked Arcadian prison guards."

"Well." Doyle dips a deferential nod. "That'll wash as good enough."

"And *your* laundry isn't just as dirty?"

Doyle turns from him—not aware I've come closer. At least close enough to see the thunder in his eyes as he all but whispers, "They had to burn my laundry, man."

He clearly wants to let that go; so I do. Besides, I have a bigger priority. Making sure I hug as much of my gratitude into them both as possible.

But the next second, even that is shifted to a back burner.

A far one.

How can I focus on anything but the electric change in the air. No...the physical shifting of its molecules, funneling to shoot a jolt of awareness down my spine equaling no other...

Possible because of no one else...

But him.

Cassian.

I do not even want to speak it, for fear of shattering the spell and rendering this joy into just another dream. Instead I turn, letting the tired but perfect beauty of him fill my gaze, explode my heart...and compel my body. I lunge into his arms, letting him lift me up and fold me close. Though his grip is as powerful as ever, I feel the creep of exhaustion through his body. Smell the tang of dirt roads, night wind, and sea spray on his still-moist skin. As if I care. The man could have rolled in a damn pig's trough, and I *would not care.*

"Armeau." His voice is like the sea too, a roll of liquid thunder through us both. Never would I think it possible for the sound to touch deeper parts of me, but it does, vibrating through every fiber...

Until I am lost in him once more.

Lost *to* him...

"You are really safe." I rasp it into his neck.

"Yeah."

"You are really here."

"Yeah." His stance stiffens. He lowers me in order to push me back by a few inches. "And so are you."

Uh-oh.

His disappointment—his anger—are real; I see that much in the emerald accusation of his gaze. But accepting them as *valid* is a separate struggle.

And, if I am being utterly honest, an unnecessary one.

"Cassian."

"Mishella." His concluding lilt carries an edge of warning. He has not invoked my middle name, but I wonder how close *that* came to happening. Higher instinct tells me to be afraid, but I simply am not.

I am just as irate as he is.

"No." I yank back, bracing hands to my hips. "You will *not* turn me contrite about this." Jerk a look back toward Damon and Doyle. "Nor will you blame either of them for it. I did not even tell them about your order, so they cannot be held—"

"I know."

The new calm in his voice is unnerving. "You do?"

"He does." Oh. *There* is the accusation. In *Doyle's* voice.

Shit.

"Damn right he does." Damon's too.

Shit, shit, *shit.*

Cassian slides a hand against one of mine. The move is not one of tenderness—even mercy. "And you're right, little girl. I'll hold neither of *them* responsible for *your* actions."

Hard swallow.

And a resolute jerk of my chin.

And an utter gauntlet of a glare, meeting the challenge of his.

"Do you really want to do this *now*?" I hiss.

Why does the appearance of his dimples suddenly make my nerves feel like ice picks? I refuse acknowledge the answer. He refuses to let me do anything else. "Now's a damn good time, armeau. Yes."

"Fine," I snap. "But it was the right call. I was able to help, and I am not going to be sorry about it."

The dimples disappear. Maybe that is because the other men's chuckles—even Samsyn's—take over on the nerve-grating duties. "'Not sorry' can be turned into 'please let me be sorry' very quickly, little one," the prince murmurs.

"Or very slowly," Doyle adds.

"Gah." Damon glowers. "You two want to cool that shit? You're talking about my baby brother."

None of their jibes are as intimidating as Cassian's calm concession to them. As if they are not jokes at all, but...

But what?

My trepidation is not eased as he lifts a stare toward Samsyn. "How long can you give me?"

I sprint a glance between them. "Give you for what?"

"I would estimate an hour," Samsyn supplies as if I have not said a thing. "Maybe ninety minutes. My last update on the road closure was just five minutes ago. I have ordered the lockdown for another hour and can keep it that way for a little while longer. After that, things will start to look suspicious."

"Road closure?" I officially run the risk of appearing like an idiot parrot but am beyond concern for that as well. Clearly, details of his escape from Censhyr have included details beyond what I helped facilitate—and since they directly impact a commodity as precious as time, I will readily embrace the parrot. "Road to where? And why is it closed?"

Cassian dips his gaze to me, maintaining his odd cloak of calm. Lifts a hand, long-fingered and still a little damp, to the space between my hair and nape. "The coastal road, to the airport," he states. "And they've closed it because they're looking for the guy who escaped from Censhyr—whom they suspect will make a run for his jet."

His tone is far from censuring. It does not have to be. He

respects my mind too much—what he knows I will be able to infer now—to clobber me with anvils of accusation.

My own psyche does *that* job just fine.

Before remembering that I am *not* sorry about this.

"Well. Their searches will be for naught then, hmm?"

"For now." Once again, it is underlined with tight calm. As if he is guarding part of himself. No. Not "as if." He is hiding something from me...

But what?

And why?

"For now?" I bite it out. "What does *that* mean?"

"Exactly what he means, Mishella." Samsyn's tone possesses the same careful weirdness. "That the road is closed—until logically, we cannot keep it closed any longer. At that point, the search for Cassian will tighten...and likely focus on Sancti."

I have refused to veer my stare from Cassian. Until now. "Sancti," I fire at Samsyn. "And the palais? *Here?*"

He wastes no time with extra actions to confirm it. "Where they will also find nothing."

Cassian squeezes my nape tighter. "Because by that time, the escapee *will* be on the road to the airport."

"Smuggled out in a truck of secured cargo." Samsyn includes Doyle and Damon in the sweep of a look he tags to his insertion. "Driven by a pair of crazy-ass soldiers with the bushiest eyebrows in the Mediterranean."

Doyle snorts. "Careful, bucko. You're biting off some big territory there."

"Then be prepared to live up to it," Syn rebuts.

"Just call us Mario and Luigi."

"Who and who?"

"Dude." Damon grimaces. "We'd need the mustaches again for that."

"Yeah," Doyle concedes. "And hats. If you're going to do the Bros, you gotta have the hats."

Cassian's face contorts between a laugh and a glower. "I have no idea whether to punch or thank you guys for invoking the Mario at a time like this."

"Thank us."

"Punch us."

The tandem answer may inspire chuffs from Cassian and Samsyn, but I am *not* on the humor train—or fooled by it. I show Cassian as much by pivoting sharply in his hold—and sweeping up a scythe of a stare. "All right," I charge. "Pause button. *Now.*" That earns me his renewed focus, eyes intense as twin lasers. That is good. Very good. I think. "What the hell is really going on?" I demand. "What are you *not* telling me?"

Very good swings swiftly to *very bad.*

If Cassian's stillness is not my first clue, the three other men become his disturbingly quiet lieutenants. Finally, Samsyn utters, "Better take this to the other room."

Cassian exhales with deliberation. "You're probably right."

"The other room?" I resort to darting glances back and forth between them again. "What? Why?"

"It is *fine*, Cassian," Syn reassures. "I will come knock when it is time."

Cassian lingers a second longer. Another. I wonder why *I* suddenly feel like the caged lion here—and he has become the poor sot assigned to step inside the bars with me. "Thanks, Syn." He resecures his hand against mine before tugging me into the bedroom where we slept last night. The command in his guidance is *not* to be brooked.

The second we are inside and he closes the door, I confront him head on, air-quoting Samsyn's words as an accusation. "'When it is time?' And 'better take this to the other room?'" When he issues no response except a harsher set of his jaw, I persist, "Cassian...*dammit*. Talk to me. Is he going to be returning with a bloody firing squad in tow?"

I wish like hell I could fling it as more of a joke.

That he would smirk, taking it as one.

That he would do anything but hook both my hands into his, pulling in a deep, resigned breath—deep-freezing my heart already for what is *not* going to be a jest of an answer.

Shit.

Shit.

Shit.

"Because in an hour, he's coming to get us, Ella. Then we're sneaking out of here in that truck, and I'm going to put you on the jet with Damon and Doyle. And then Samsyn is taking me back to Censhyr, where I'll turn myself back in."

CHAPTER EIGHT

CASSIAN

For a strange second, I ponder who's taught her how to slap so well.

There's real talent to this kind of shit—especially connecting hard enough to ring a guy's ears. I'd actually be impressed, if I wasn't busy forcing the neurons in my brain to reconnect.

"Are you out of your bloody mind?"

Now that you bring it up...

"Armeau—"

"Stop." She whirls so swiftly, her hair whips across my chest. Three stomps in, and she spins back around, slicing me with the fresh tears in her eyes and the desperation on her face. "You do not get to 'armeau' me into submission right now. You do not get to shut me out of the damn conversation. I will not stand for it like I did yesterday!"

Scowl. Deep. As in, I'm sure my face has some new permanent grooves now. "Yesterday? What the *hell* about yest—"

"You? My mother? My father?" she snarls. "Sealed off, signing more contracts that landed you in *this* very position?"

"Which would have made all of it worse, because you'd now be an accessory." I pull in a deep breath. Drop my head and squeeze the bridge of my nose. "Above and beyond that, Ella, you are *done* with the poison of your parents—"

"*You* do not get to decide that!"

"The hell I don't. When their bullshit affects *your* happiness and prosperity—"

"My prosperity?" She lifts it to a yell. "My prosperity, dammit, is *you*." After another growl, swings a hand against the bedpost with an audible *smack*. "And *you* do *not* get to stand there and shatter my heart—my fucking soul!—*again*, and be Mr. Calm, Suave, and fucking Sophisticated about it!"

I take a step. She shoves against the bedpost, widening the space between us.

Shit.

"Is that what you think?" My riposte is so steeled, I wonder how a choke chain hasn't appeared around my neck. "Seriously? God*dam*mit, Ella—do you truly think I'm just chillin' with 'suave' and 'sophisticated' over here? That I've even invited Chantal Dunne and her crew down to record everything because I'll look so fucking *suave* saying goodbye to the woman I love for God knows how long?"

Not. Smart.

I know it before the fresh blue blaze in her eyes. Bringing up the gossip TV reporter who outed our relationship to the world two weeks ago is close to knocking her down and then booting her in the gut.

"I'm...sorry," I mutter. "But if you think—"

"No." Her locked teeth flash at me. "No, Cassian, you are not sorry."

I approach her again. This time, I don't care how quickly she scrambles back. There's only so much space in this room. "Know what, armeau? Maybe you're right." Tightened jaw.

Gaze full of triumph as she backs against an overstuffed chair centered in front of the bay window. The furniture is positioned perfectly, with panoramic views of the sea and the sweeping cliffs of the island's south coast. Right now, I don't care if Atlantis itself is exposed. My concentration is consumed, solely and selfishly, on the woman now just inches away. "Yeah. Maybe you're *exactly* right. Maybe, ultimately, I'm just a selfish prick. Maybe I have been from the start."

She blinks rapidly. Shakes as if fighting off a shiver. "Th-That's not what I said."

"No. It's what I said." I press in on her by half a step. "What I *am* saying."

Both her hands rise to my chest. They're still wound into fists. We both note it. "Cassian—"

"We wouldn't be here right now, in this exact fuck fest, if it wasn't for me and my selfishness." I wrap a hand around one of hers. Then the other. Make it impossible for her to uncoil her fingers, despite the twitches betraying how she wants to...

To soothe me.

Touch me.

No. I don't get to have that right now. God*damm*it, I should have never seized the right to have *her*.

"You haven't thought of that, have you?" I grate. "You haven't considered that if I wasn't a cocky sonofabitch, so used to having and getting my way, that three days after meeting you, I walked into your parents' villa carrying the contract that told them I meant to have you. That I'd *pay* for you, like some prize mare at auction—"

"Stop." She wrestles harder against me. Struggles to be free—to fight me for *my* fucking honor. The woman can't see that what little I have will soon be devoured by wolves—and that even if those last scraps are an unfair kill, *I'm* the one who supplied the original knife for the slaughter. "Stop it," she hisses. "Or I will, Creator help me!"

"Great idea." Fury and frustration hit the override switch at once. I release her with a vicious shove. "Yeah. Fucking awesome idea. You let your Creator help you, Mishella, because right now, *I can't.*"

She keeps her hands balled against her chest. They rise and fall with her desperate breaths. "Sure. That makes all the sense in the world. Because you did nothing to help me by breaking out of prison, only so you could make sure I get back on the damn plane—and fly to the safety you deny *yourself?*"

"Running from this *would be* denial." I drop my hands. Fist them, battling the urge to rush back to her. To ease this brutal blow by touching her, holding her. But where's that going to take us both in another hour—except further down the chasm of pain and heartache? For once, my dick or my heart can't dictate my actions. There's too much at stake. "I'd have eight hours with you on the plane—enough time for the CIA to round up their evidence, hand it over to the FBI, and then watch while I'm formally arrested as soon as we land at Teterboro."

Blue diamonds chase each other in her gaze as the gears in her brain clearly churn. Two seconds after she looks back up, she's a rushing fullback, curvy Arcadian style. "So we do not land at Teterboro." Her grip is actually strong enough to seize pigskin, as she grabs up my hands again. "Cassian, *please.* Laith will take the plane anywhere we want; you know he will. We can go to Los Angeles or Miami or Kalamazoo—"

"Kalamazoo?" Dear hell. How this woman curates the shit in her gray matter is a constant surprise—and joy.

The diamonds dance now, joyous and sparkling, jolting straight to my cock despite every shitty aspect of this situation. "Have you ever been there?"

"Can't say I have."

"Good. Me neither. So we go see Kalamazoo, then drive all over Michigan, and then—"

I silence her with a kiss. It's quick, nearly sterile, but I don't want to let her hands go. So much for resisting the temptation of her touch. Or anything else about her. "Drive all over Michigan...in what? And stay where? And eat what while we do?" I counter gently. "The second I use a credit card or need to access money, they'll know where I'm at, armeau—and they'll have local law enforcement swooping in on me. And before you go for international options"—because I can see *that* light already sparking across her face—"remember they are the *CIA*. They can close in on me over foreign soil with even scarier speed."

Her mouth opens. Clamps shut again. Right before fresh wells of tears brim in her eyes—and she jumps *my* shit with a kiss too.

But the contact isn't clinical. Or tender.

It's a push, a punishment, almost an attack. An outpouring of her fear, needing to spill out as her fight, mixed in with the passion and fire and purpose of her love.

And I let her come. As hard, as thorough, and as brutally as she needs. Fuck, I probably even welcome it. Need it. Crave it as a surrogate for the raging frustration and helpless defeat with which I've struggled for the last two hours—endured, over and over again, as I've reviewed all the details of what information the Feds can possibly have enough of to come sniffing with even a hint of charges in this mess. Knowing what they *do* have has absolutely been twisted, reinterpreted, even doctored to skew my innocence.

Knowing that right now, on this island in the middle of nowhere, I'm impotent to do a goddamn thing about it.

"Is there not...any other way?"

And in my mind sounding a hell of a lot like that—only without a husky Arcadian accent. And injected with a few more profanities. Maybe more than a few.

Either way, the woman succeeds, as usual, in scooping thoughts out of my head and right into the center of hers—but then taking them deeper. Weaving them into herself, making them part of her breath, her blood, her soul...and then making me a part of them all too.

And in doing so, healing me.

Restoring me.

Completing me.

Do I do the same for her? The question tears at my gut and claws toward my throat, straining to be voiced. I swallow it down. I already know what she'd say—and even thinking of not being here for her already burns my blood like battery acid. Worse. My mind. And my soul.

Especially because I can feel her parents in the very air.

Her parents—who are not done with her by half.

They're simply biding their damn time. Waiting for me to be out of the picture once more before descending upon her like killer bees on a blooming rose, ready to strip out her life without care for the destruction they leave behind.

"Cassian." Her plea cuts into me—through me—along with the desperate curl of her fingers into the front of my shirt. The contact suffuses me with enough warmth to have made the decision worth it. *All* of the decision. Even the part I still have yet to face...

"*Please*, Cassian." She pulls harder. "Is there *not* any other way?" Her gaze rakes my face. "Any other plan we can consider?" Her fingers follow, tracing the lines of my face through my stubble, spreading to bracket the corners of my eyes. "Any corner of the world we can go...and just *be*?"

For an instant, maybe two, the yearning to nod becomes another choke chain. Resistance becomes a strangle. A *yes* pushes at my lips so violently, my entire jaw aches from holding it back. I grab her closer, ordering myself to focus on the feel of her, the warmth of her, the beautiful island smell of her. This, *all* of this, is what's going to get me through the hell of what's to come.

"Cassian?"

Before I can succumb, I shake my head. Shove words out. The right words—spoken with every scrap of my pride and strength. *I am the subject of nobody's pity.*

"No, raismette." I tug her closer, fitting her head atop my heartbeat. "We're not going to go anywhere."

She jerks back. Glares up in a mix of supplication and accusation. "Because we cannot?" she levels. "Or because *you* will not?"

Heavy exhalation. "Because I refuse to turn you into a goddamn fugitive."

"What if that is not your call to make?"

"What if that's a shitty card to throw?" I ride out her anger, as tangible as a fireball on the air, more than ready with a counterblast. "Let me be completely clear, Mishella DaLysse." I anchor a thumb beneath her chin. "You are *mine*—and I will never hide it. Because of that, you'll never hide, either. You will *not* skulk around in some shithole corner of the globe, having to worry about every stranger turning you in, looking over your shoulder every time you so much as step outside the door."

She absorbs that with a shaky sigh. "But what if—"

"You want that life?" I damn near snarl it. "No. You *don't* want it. You don't want it because that is not who you are, dammit. It is not the woman I first met in that reception hall downstairs two months ago, or the person I glimpsed in beautiful little spurts over the three days after that, or the goddess worth scaling a trellis for, just to steal one perfect kiss."

I add a forefinger to my grip. Yank her face a little higher. My heart jerks too—into the center of my throat. She is so fucking beautiful. Her flawless skin, now bathed in shades of moon glow, is contrasted by the silver-kissed lagoons in her eyes.

Finally, I state, "It sure as hell isn't the woman who stood before me in her parents' villa, willing to sign away six months of her life in exchange for a life of freedom—*not* a life of secrecy, pretense, and double truths."

Her eyes shimmer brighter. The thick tears threaten to brim over. Her chin juts against my hold, defiant and adorably obstinate. "The only truth I need is you."

"I know," I grate. "But the truth you *deserve* is much more." I lift my thumb, tracing the bottom edge of her lip. Committing her soft, smiling bravery to every corner of my memory. "You deserve a life of fulfillment and laughter, of joy and excitement and beauty." I shift closer to her because I'm fucking unable to help myself—and getting inside the bubble with her, just one more time, feels too perfect. Completely, irrevocably right. "You deserve to have breakfast every morning up on the terrace. To wander flea markets on Saturdays and stay in bed half the day on Sundays. You deserve to help Scott tinker with the cars, to go to the spa with Kate and then taunt me with your newly waxed 'sweet parts,' until you wake me up in the middle of the night to watch a storm roll down the Hudson from our special spot up in the turret..."

Shit.

You had *to bring up the turret, asshole?*

My self-edit is much too late. Ella's violent sway and silent sob are my punishment. A violent breath into her hair is a piss-poor apology, especially because I hardly mean it. If I'm going to end this night in a jail cell, I'll selfishly grab a memory as a goodbye gift: the vision of our first night in that tower—one of her first in Manhattan—when we'd watched such a storm take over the city before letting the electricity take over our minds, spirits, and bodies.

I'd been inside her for the first time that night.

A magic we've never duplicated...

...because every time we fuck, it gets even better...

and better...

and better...

She kisses me again, turning this moment into an example that's completely exquisite...

and erotic...

and eternal...

and unlike any mesh of our mouths I've ever experienced.

Holy. Fuck.

She pulls me down harder, twisting my hair and scoring my skin, returning the stabs of my tongue with ferociousness and fury. Her needy mewl turns into a thousand sparks in my blood. Her desperate touch ignites pure fire in its wake.

I'm so stunned, I almost stop.

Almost.

Where is my little Arcadian courtier? The maid with the flowery wall of reserve I always like seducing out of the way, often through *very* creative wickedness? The girl with the face of a Victorian cameo, the panties of a pin-up virgin, and the mind of a sweet temptress—all of which she celebrates, every time she relinquishes them to me.

Completely.

Irretrievably.

So fucking beautifully...

Even now.

Especially now.

I swear to God, she's never taken my breath away more than this instant, peering up at me with eyes so dusky and lusty, cheeks so flushed and hot, and that delectable corner of her mouth, caught beneath her teeth...knowing exactly what kind of impact it has on my psyche. And my cock.

And I was actually *missing* the court maiden...why?

"You know I do not care about scones on the terrace, right?"

"Huh?"

Christ. I never knew *she* knew how to drop her shoulder like that. Or that her slouchy pink sweater could slip down that low when she did...exposing the top of her breast. Stretching the knit fabric across her chest, to define the other swell so perfectly. Even ensuring that nipple poked at the woven threads, urgently enough to taunt me.

She smiles softly.

My blood roars. My dick throbs. My fantasies prepare to declare war on my psyche, and the damn woman *smiles* like she's about to go enjoy a scone on the fucking terrace. But the scones don't matter. That *is* what she said, right?

"No scones."

She husks it like an answer to my mind's question, adding a sultrier version of that damn smile. That smile is...dangerous. Part of me yearns to wipe it off her face. Another part wants to know what it'll develop into. Neither bode well for the torture still calling itself my dick.

"No scones," she repeats. "Or spa trips. Or tinkering with the cars. But maybe"—she sets her lip free, only to wet the surface with the gorgeous nub of her tongue—"I still need Sundays in bed." She squirms a little, sliding the sweater over her body in astonishing new ways. "I suppose it would depend on what our plans were."

I plunge my gaze into hers. The savage grip of her fear is clear in those bright-blue depths—as well as her determination to distract us both from it with this little sex kitten act.

And fuck me, it's working.

No. If we're going to spend our last hour twined and naked with each other, I need to trade out Wolverine for Captain America. Give her a sweet, meaningful screw, not a panting, dog breath ball-beater.

A plan even she seems hell-bent on cock-blocking. Figuratively speaking—

Or not.

A groan thunders up my body as she palms the stalk between my legs—and then strokes up, gripping me from balls to crown, claiming with the boldness of intention. Lots of it. Wanton and possessive—and perfect.

"I think," she murmurs, once more with that flirty grin, "I would have some definite plans...for Sundays in bed with this."

I let one of my hands drop. Capture her wrist with it. Lift it to my mouth and capturing it in a relentless suckle. Take my turn to unfurl a smile as her lips part on an unthinking gasp.

Maybe Captain America's overrated.

"What if I had a few plans of my own?"

Her chest pumps as I continue nibbling...marking a path toward her inner elbow. Christ, what that does to the sweater—and the evidence of her arousal, now two distinct points beneath the pink covering. I stare at them, hard. She notices, and they get harder.

"P-Plans?" she finally sputters—and just like that, my wide-eyed princess is back, ready to let me steal her white panties...and lure away all her inhibitions. The timing couldn't be better. I slide my lips up, over her shoulder and then against her neck, nipping as I did at her wrist, making her gasp twice as loud.

Damn...yes...

"Yes," I finish to her query. "Only they may or may not involve a bed." Because even the five steps to get *there* are too huge a journey to contemplate. In two, we can make it to the big chair in the curve of the bay window...

And we do.

A nudge of my foot behind her ankles, and she'll be perfectly sprawled in the middle of it, spreading her legs as I descend over her...

And she is.

Just a couple of strategic pushes, taking advantage of the slack in her sweater now...

And...

Yeah.

"Yesssss." It hisses from me, rough and ruthless as the desire rising through me, as I drink in the perfection of her taut, dusky nipples.

Shit.

"Yesssss."

For a long minute, that's all I'm capable of getting out. The word escapes between my licks at her erect tips, a prayer of thanksgiving *and* agony, as I taste, tantalize, and tease us both into a tumult of need, heat, and lust. The rips of pain through my skull, brought on by her urgent tugs on my hair, are her way of adding to the torment. Every time she twists, I close down tighter on her incredible breasts.

"Damn!" She cries it out as I lift to assess—admire?—the damage.

"Damn."

Yeah. It's admiration.

I've outdone myself.

Her gorgeous tits are a patchwork of red and pink, her nipples berry-red from my bites, her flesh swollen with the marks of my possession, abraded from the scrape of my beard. I want to find a paintbrush and sign my damn name.

"Christ, Ella." I grab my crotch. Openly squeeze myself in front of her. It's the only way to keep my erection in check. "You're a masterpiece."

She leans back, angling deeper against the chair. Throws up her hands, threading through her curls as she does, fanning their dark-gold light against the dark leather. "I am *your* masterpiece."

I lean forward. Shove her sweater up and over her head. I have *not* overlooked the fact that all she's worn with the thing are a pair of patterned leggings—so those get peeled off too. And—*fuck yes*—the lace-trimmed panties underneath them.

After tossing the clothes to the floor, I brace over her. Grit against the yearning to savor this moment for much,

much longer. To roam my hands over every creamy inch of her nudity, watching my touch affect her in tiny shivers, larger tremors, and finally in undulating need. To tell *her* what she does to me in return...in explicit detail. To unleash the filthy creature in her that doesn't just crave me in return for it...but loves me for it.

But we're a cyclone in a bubble. With every passing moment, our magic shell stretches thinner.

I rip at my fly. Let myself out. Let her gaze fall to the length in my hand as I fist the last few spasms of arousal up into my length.

My slit spurts, giving me a slicker surface to work with. The scent of it hits Ella, and her face suffuses with need. Her lip disappears between her teeth again. Pops back out because she bites so damn hard. Good. That's *so* good. I want her as agonized as me. As tortured, as pain-ridden...as driven to the brink of her very sanity from this need...from craving our connection.

Please, armeau. Stay connected...

Be here for me.

Just like this for me.

Exactly this soaked for me.

Holy. Fuck.

I hardly realize it's growled out of me until her gaze bulges, searching me. Hating myself for bringing her even those two seconds of pain, I crash a devouring kiss to her mouth. But stop there? No chance. I push deeper, swiping my tongue totally in, dominating her.

When we finally drag apart, I whip off my shirt. Drop back down to poise over her by just a few inches. To impose my heat on her. Brand my stare into her.

Position my cock to impale her.

"You're perfect. Dear God, Ella...in more ways than I ever could dream."

"Cassian." She lifts a hand, angling it to cup my face. I halt it halfway, locking it back down against the cushion beside her head. Pin down the other in the exact same way. Needing her like this. Needing to feel, at least once in this fucked twist of my life, in complete control.

Seeing that understanding in her eyes. In the lift of her face. In the arch of her breasts.

Fuck.

She doesn't just get it. She wants it, too. Yearns to give it all to me. All of *herself* to me.

The realization brings another with it...just as perfect. Now more than ever, I want her for the rest of my life. To *be* my life. To stand before me in a wedding gown, raise her head with that exact smile on her face, and become my woman for the rest of our years...

And if the rest of your years are behind steel bars?

I can't ignore the possibility. Can't stuff down the fact that I'm about to willingly turn myself over to people who could have me branded as a terrorist—a traitor to my country, a murderer to hers—inside a week. That inside that same week, I might be stowed away in some cell, in the middle of some desert, awaiting a trial that will never take place...

Then make this count, asshole.

Make. Her. Remember.

The mandate is a shaft of sun, funneling the focus of all my darkness. In the middle of that sun, there is only Ella. Only the brilliance of our bubble. Only the blinding, blazing importance of making my life into this now...my world into this woman.

With that thought consuming my mind, I sink my lips against hers. Push deeper inside. Taste her. Devour her.

Conquer her.

My arousal grows as my control slips. Precariously. My pants drop down to my calves, and I kick them free. As I press harder over her, my world narrows even more. I kiss her with everything I have, everything I am. Vow to pleasure her with all the force of my passion and power of my body. Comprehending, at last, why Arcadian men run right past all our stupid American names for our women and turn to the only one that makes real sense.

"Raismette."

Though it is the highest honor I can give her, I issue it as full command—because it's what she craves too. What she needs. To be pulled out of her high heels, swept off her feet, and then pinned on her back, wrapped in the fullness of desire... claimed by her male's ruling hand.

She drags her eyes open. Their depths are as fathomless as the sea outside, as perfect as the stars reflecting over those waves. Then she smiles, her lips curved with understanding... and gratitude.

And surrender.

"Yes, Cassian?"

I lower my head, only brushing my lips to hers now. "Open for me." A growl of approval as her thighs part—and mine slide between them. "Damn. So good."

"Yes, Cassian." It's agreement this time, not acquiescence.

"Wider. Get your ankles onto both sides." I groan low as she complies, spreading her intimate lips to accommodate my pulsing tip. Her body starts sucking me in, all but begging me to invade her tight channel. The perfection of it makes us both shudder—bodies fitting, breaths tangling, hearts joining. "Good, favori. God*damn*."

"Yes." Her wrists twist in my hold—but not fighting me. Needing me. The tension of the fight... It's what we both need in order to drag out the magnificence of our pleasure. "Yes, Cassian!"

My buttocks clench. My thighs tremble. The craving to sink in is so fucking intense—and soon, so very soon, I'll indulge it. It's everything I want but everything I hate, for the moment I'm buried inside her is one moment closer to having to pull out—and prepare to say goodbye to her.

"Your cunt wants me, Ella."

"It—it does, Cassian."

"It's so wet. So perfect. This sweet little body, made just for me."

"Just...for you." Tears tinge her words, but so does the rattle and gasp of raw desire.

"And my cock has been made to fuck it. To fill it."

"Yes, Cassian. Only you."

"To...hurt you."

"Yes. *Yes*."

I dip in. Just a little. Can't help it. The heat of her walls surrounds my head, milking the final drops of my precome. My balls clench, preparing the massive flood that will follow.

So soon now...

Dear God, what she does to me...

I stave the inevitable by rolling my hips. Ella cries out, her back arching and muscles straining as I expected they would. The Creator has wired her in miraculous ways, including the sensitivity to this kind of stimulation, making it a breathtaking experience to torment her like this. Especially when I give her the words to go with it.

"Your pussy is trembling for me, Ella."

"It—it is, Cassian."

"Tell me why, armeau. All of it."

"It—my pussy—it...wants you, Cassian."

"Needs me?"

"Yes. Needs you."

"To do what?"

"To fuck it. To fuck *me*." She writhes, her body burning, coiling, tightening beneath me, around me. I'm not even all the way in, and my gorgeous little conquest has become my captor—as usual. "By the *Creator*. Dammit, Cassian. *Please...*"

Though my body bellows with need and my cock registers me for the *Most Wanted* list, I shower her with a cocky grin. "I could listen to you say that a hundred more times."

A delicious snarl bursts from her clenched teeth. "Let me up. *Please*. I need to touch you—"

"You *are* touching me." I undulate my hips. Feed a little more of my shaft into her welcoming depths.

"Cassian! Dammit!"

"Uh-uh." I'm not gloating about it anymore—and emphasize the point by plunging my stare into hers. "You'll agree with me now because you didn't before." I let her see it all now. The love. The need. And yeah, even the pain. Maybe that most of all. "When I found out you hadn't gotten on the plane—that as I sat in that prison, your parents were roaming free, probably plotting to get their claws back into you—"

"But they did not." The little sneak tests my grip, actually checking to see if my agony has weakened me. If she were thinking clearly, she'd remember I've built my life on being strong through my pain—of channeling it into my greatest ally.

"And they *will not*, Cassian."

"Damn straight they won't." I hunch in, sealing the vow with a tongue lashing of a kiss. "Because you're going to mind me this time, dammit. You're going to get on that airplane, still reeling from being fucked by me. You're going to walk up those stairs, every inch of your pussy still sore and stretched by me. Every breath you take will smell of me. Every corner of your womb will still carry my come."

"Oh." It's a sparse rasp. Her face is no longer terse. Her eyes, wide and bright, are a spectrum of new color. Her lips part, shiny from being wetted by her furtive tongue. "Oh...*my*."

She's the most incredible thing I've ever seen.

Making all my instincts roar in erotic glory.

"What the hell does that mean?" In any other scenario, I'd never ask something so coarse—but every inch of her face shows that she gets this. Knows my needs as blatantly as I grasp hers. That in this moment, lines must be drawn more brutally between us. "Tell me *clearly*, Ella. Tell me you understand."

She jerks out a swift nod. "Yes, Cassian. I—I understand."

I sweep inside her, deeper and harder. I'm almost there, buried to the hilt in her cunt. Her walls tremble, struggling to accommodate my fullness.

"You understand...that I'm going to fuck you hard."

"Yes," she rasps. "You're going to fuck me hard."

"And you're going to let me."

"And...and I'm going to let you."

"And you're going to hurt."

"Yes, Cassian."

I slam in, making her body take me fully. She winces, not expecting the lunge.

I rejoice.

I don't want to torture her. But goddamn, I need to master her. Mark her from the inside out, with fearlessness she will get from no other lover. That even if they lock me up and throw away the key, this woman will live the rest of her days remembering the night I claimed her without restraint... without repentance.

Triumph consumes. Powers the force of my thrusts, the brutality of my grip—the heights of her cries. She's trapped, open, helpless—and aroused as hell. I stare into her eyes, dominated by her dilated pupils. I stroke the crazy dance of her pulse. And I keep fucking her, the brutal passion growing into relentless stabs, her slick body trembling for more and more.

"*Katansi, ma dinné.*"

Take me, woman.

"Yes, ma donné."

Yes, my man.

"Deeper, Ella."

"Yes, Cassian!"

Fuck. *Fuck.* She turns me into fire. Lightning. Spears of light and feeling, lust and arousal, beyond anything I've ever fathomed possible in my body before...

Because I'd never dreamed this completion would be possible for my soul.

This freedom for my heart.

This ecstasy...in every single cell of my being.

"My armeau." My unexpected gift from heaven. My sweet, hot toy of a woman. "I'm going to fill you, Mishella. Take my come. *All of it.*"

She gives me no answer. Only her scream, wild and perfect and shattered, as her tunnel squeezes around me and her clit vibrates against my lower belly. My balls react, tensing and tightening before launching the rush of perfect heat straight up my cock. Then my consciousness is nothing but my essence, streams of life bursting into her, drenching all of her. My vision blurs and my body shakes, overcome by the need to keep scorching her, marking her, being whole and perfect and one with her.

The only element that finally yanks me free...is her. More specifically, her tears, softly shed as I ease into a gentle rocking instead of a brutal pounding. I'm not sure that helps. I stay inside her as long as I can, releasing my hold to wrap her close. Let her rise up to clutch me in return.

The wind flows in, spiced with sea salt and night mists, cooling the sweat on our flesh but binding the gentle passion of our new kiss. It's slow and deep and cherishing—and exactly what I need to give her as thanks for the caveman claim I've just made on her body.

After long minutes, I force myself to let at least a few practical thoughts back in. After pulling out of her, I stand. She giggles as I wobble for a second, really not sure my ass won't be kissing the ottoman behind my knees, but my legs finally cooperate, and I lope to the bathroom for a towel to clean us up.

When I reenter the bedroom, I'm pleased as hell to see she hasn't found it necessary to budge. Not an inch. I make my way back toward her...

But am stopped short halfway.

Struck by a feeling so rare and sublime, I almost feel ten years old again.

Yeah, ten.

That had to be the last time I stopped myself for the sake of sheer beauty.

Fuck. She doesn't just halt my steps. She seizes my whole damn heart. Moonlight streams in, a creamy caress over her skin. Her fingers flow, graceful and slow, through her thick curls. There's blue starlight love in her eyes and crevices of sexy mystery in every curve of her body. Mysteries I've just unlocked yet already lust to do so again.

I have got to be the luckiest fucker on the planet.

And the stupidest.

It's not too late.

I swallow hard. Lock my teeth. Fight the demon on one of my shoulders. He's a nasty little asshole. But why is he naked?

Because I'm you, dumb shit.

And now I'm ordering you to get the fuck over yourself. It's not too late. *Get her up, get her dressed, and get her out of here. She was right, you know. Laith will fly you two anywhere. He'll even help in finding the perfect hiding spot. Some remote island in the middle of nowhere, where neither of you will need clothes and everyone pays for food with songs or pebbles. You can run around in a loincloth for the rest of your days and fuck your beautiful Ella every damn chance you can get...*

And that would do *what* to Mom? And Prim? And the thousands of people who depend on me for *their* chance at loincloths and pebble payments?

I chose my life. I *made* my life.

And that meant choosing not to run, just because doing the right thing meant doing the hard thing.

But right now...this moment...

There is just savoring the beauty.

"What on earth are you thinking?"

And loving her for seeing into me like a laser through a diamond—but asking that question anyway.

"You already know that answer, armeau."

A misty smile lights up her lips. "Perhaps I do."

"Then you probably know I'm just enjoying the view." Deep rush of an inhalation. "And memorizing it."

The smiles vanishes. "Cassian." Her beckoning hand matches the urgency of her whisper. "My raismette."

Her plea gets me moving again. Though there's enough room to sit next to her on the chair, I kneel instead. I need this—to physically show her how deep I shall always be in service to her.

How I will never forget the perfect gift of her...

And yeah, it's fun to make her squirm again. Just a little. Number one, the pause helps me resist the temptation to pleasure her again. Number two—*paging Hypocrites Anonymous*—I get to appreciate what impatience does to her luscious little body.

"Hold still." I give the quiet command when stroking into the curve of her knee—just as she tries to wriggle free.

She flings a teasing glower. "Cad. You know I am ticklish there."

"A fact I learned *long* after you knew I was a cad."

She sighs, a combination of dreamy and resigned, as I dip a kiss to the inside of her kneecap. With the pad of my thumb, I rub the same place on her opposite knee. "You have ruined me for cads, Mr. Court."

"You're ruined only for *this* fucking cad, Miss Santelle."

She twines a huskier breath with my unexpected snarl. "Yes, sir." Lifts a hand into my hair, compelling me to take in every inch of the stunning smile she joins to it. "Only you. Always."

Again, I'm speechless. Unable to give her the reply she

deserves—the answer that's *right*—to tell her I can't accept her promise, no matter how deep from her being it has emerged. That I can't ask her to wait for me, if the Feds make this bullshit stick and then ruin me for it. I will *not* do that to her.

But those words aren't the ones that form. Though I surge to my feet and turn from her, they aren't the vow I can muster. Nowhere near the selflessness I'm capable of.

Right now, I continue in the key of cad—and make damn certain I claim a part of her that belongs to no other.

Like writing up a contract with her companionship as a bargaining chip wasn't enough?

Then taking her virginity...that also wasn't enough?

Then falling in love with her and proposing to her...

How much of this woman is going to be enough *for you, dammit?*

"Shut up." Though I keep it as low a growl as I can, it drives Ella to her feet too. But maybe it's not the words at all. Maybe she just notices that I've stalked across the room like a man possessed. Maybe she just knows that I am.

"Cassian?"

I don't say a thing while stomping to my suitcase, a small roller bag perched next to hers, on top of the dresser. Still nothing as I flip it open and reach inside.

"Cassian, what in Creator's n—"

Still nothing as I turn with the long velvet box balanced on my upturned palms. For a few seconds, I simply let her get used to the sight, though I could have a snake in my hands and likely stunned her less.

"Better than a snake," I finally mutter. *At least I hope so.*

"Wh-What?"

"Never mind."

I laugh in lieu of kissing her—which is really what I yearn to do. Dear Christ, she's so cute, shambling in her puddle of mussed and nonplussed, rocking kiss-stung lips and freshly fucked hair like no earthly goddess has a right to. *My* goddess. And this is going to seal the deal.

"Open it, Mishella."

She doesn't move.

Except to jerk up a gaze flooded with peacock-blue awe— once more not from *what* I've spoken but how I've voiced it. This time, her full name is purposeful for me. Prayerful. A conscious choice.

Just like what rests on a bed of reverent satin in this case.

"What...what is it, Cassian?"

Deep breath. Another. This wasn't the moment I'd envisioned in my head, when hurriedly stowing the box as we packed back in New York. In my fantasy, we were both on the Arcadian beach somewhere. We were both relaxed and happy, buzzed on a little wine. We were both *clothed*. But life, from Dirt Street to Wall Street, has taught me a few lessons with regular clarity, including *make a plan—and then prepare to change it*.

In this case, the change is...

Perfect.

Standing here before this woman, naked as the day I was born, I am also able to show her the bare truth of who I am—the man beneath the conference room command and the bespoke pinstripes, the guy who just wants to be *her* guy, the soul desperately and helplessly in love with hers...

And—oh, yeah—the lover who might never get a chance to be like this with her, ever again.

Here goes fucking nothing.

"Open it." Again I nudge the box toward her. She practically jumps back, looking perplexed and even a little panicked. "Ella? Why...are you..."

She cuts me off with a despairing moan. "*Cassian.*" Backhands her forehead, enticing the air itself to write off her melodrama, if it wasn't so thick with the weight of her conflict. "Why are *you*?" she suddenly seethes. "*That* was not enough?"

I follow the stab of her finger. The *that* she refers to is her diamond cuff, resting on a shelf in the armoire next to the bathroom door, beside her watch and earrings. The moments are rare when she isn't wearing all the accessories, though the bracelet has had her most faithful adherence since I gave it to her, twelve days that seem a forever ago. It was the moment just before we took our relationship public for the world on Chantal Dunne's entertainment gossip show.

Different circumstances now.

So much different.

"That was just a commemoration," I explain.

"Of what?"

"The start."

It gets a nod of satisfaction. How else do I phrase it without sounding like an ass desperate to make everything better with jewelry? I'm not *that* fuckhead—and she sure as hell isn't that woman either.

She is *the* woman.

My true love.

Which means this is going to happen, dammit—no matter what protests she hurls.

"The start? So...this is what, Cassian? The *end*?"

Yes. Even if she hurls that.

"This is"—I finally just flip the box open for her—"my heart."

The necklace, a simple oval of tiger's eye set against an antique silver filigree, isn't as flashy as the cuff—but that's part of its perfection. It's more like her: a blend of regal alloys, a perfection of royal elegance. Silver and gold, simplicity and complexity, today's serene statement representing the strength of survival, the courage of personal history.

A history she no longer has to bear alone.

I step closer, needing her to see it in my eyes. To feel it in my presence.

"Not just my heart, Mishella." I let the serrated syllables cascade over her. "But Mom's too." Gruff laugh. "Probably Damon's by now as well. Do you understand?"

For a long moment, she's quiet. Finally raises her head, searching me with avid eyes. "I—do not know."

I line up my gaze more directly with hers. "I didn't go out and buy this necklace. I'm giving it to you because you are now not just mine. You are...ours. Family."

Her nose crinkles. Her brow furrows. "What?"

I brush a thumb along her hairline. Damn. Even the word "family" is foreign—and frightening—to her.

So I must prove how much it means to *me*.

"This has been in the Court family since the nineteen thirties," I begin, "when my great-grandfather worked two jobs for nine months to pay for it."

A few of the lines disappear from her forehead, making room for her widened eyes. "*Why?*"

"Well. He was in love with a girl. My great-grandmother, Nina. He badly wanted to seal the deal—"

"Then all he needed was some sealing wax and the family crest. He had a signet somewhere, yes?"

I bite back a grin. "In this case, it means to simply make

her his wife. Clearer?"

There's her smile—bringing back my sun. "Oh, yes. Now *that* is wonderful."

"Well...yes and no. It was the Great Depression, and he didn't have enough money to buy her an engagement ring. He found a second job at night, bizarre enough in itself, even if it was shitty labor—literally." I indulge a new chuff, shaking my head from the story Mom has told me countless times. "But for almost a year, he cleaned toilets and mopped floors from eight to midnight, just to buy my grandmother the necklace she loved in a jewelry store window."

A breath rushes from her. She strokes one shaky finger down the silver chain. "Oh, my."

"He had nothing when he proposed to her, except this necklace." A smile tugs my lips—not just inspired by the story. Her reaction to it really is like sun blazing my heart...hope soaring my spirit.

"She better have said yes!"

Her teary blurt reels me closer. I take her lips in a kiss. I stay there, lingering inches away, while relaying the conclusion of the story. "They went to the justice of the peace the next week. and he accepted the necklace as one of the finest 'wedding rings' he'd ever seen."

She pulls back her hand from the chain—

To tear it at the moisture streaking her cheeks. I slip fingers down, helping her. Unable to resist touching her. Getting as many memories as I can of her...

"When the economy got better, he finally bought her a real ring," I finish. "But to generations of Courts, this has been the more meaningful way of declaring our true intentions—to the women we truly love...and need."

She drags in a quivering breath. When it releases, a new tumult of tears pours from the incredible hurricanes of her eyes. They fall into her cleavage like rain on a cream marble statue of a sacrificial virgin.

My masterpiece.

Immaculate.

Immeasurable.

Eternal.

Dear God, please. I just want to make her happy.

Admitting it...comprehending the sheer size of it...

Drives me to my knees in front of her.

But with my head still raised, I draw the necklace away from its velvet bed. Dangle it in the air between us.

"Ella. I don't know what's going to happen over the next weeks, maybe the next few years. When this is all over, I may not have a thing to my name. No jet. No cars. No manor with turrets or buildings with my name on the door."

"Cassian." She drops her head. Shakes it hard. Even, for a second, looks like she's going to slap me—even as she plummets to the floor next to me. "You daft, proud, *stupid* man. I do not *care* about the *things* that come with your name—"

"It won't be just the things." With my free hand, I cup her face. "It'll be the very integrity of my name. The core of my honor. The backbone of my professional standing—"

She cuts me off with the perfect upsweep of her lips. I don't argue the point, letting her capture my senses with her sweet berry taste, her open and urgent passion. It's a damn fine alternative to where my moroseness was going, especially when she concludes it with a smile so perfect and peaceful, I really wonder what Victorian magazine God was reading when fashioning her. Yeah, even now with her breasts crushed against my chest and her thighs softly brushing mine.

She's a flawless fantasy. The ultimate incarnation of all my damn dreams.

But never more so than when she tugs up her chin, widens her smile, and gives me a gift outshining the necklace itself.

A perfect promise of a whisper.

"Beautiful, ridiculous man. Do you not see yet? We shall never have *nothing*—because we shall always have each other."

I curl fingers back into her hair. Grip her like a lifeline. Who the hell am I kidding? She *is* my lifeline. I let her see it, feel it, know it...

Before I finally speak it.

"We will, won't we?"

Her eyes smile first, turning morning sunshine blue. "Yes, Cassian."

I smile too. Expose the full dazzle of my dimples, just the way she likes it. I relish her sexy little sigh and, for one moment, simply pretend the bubble will never break. That we can really do this.

"For better, for worse."

I blurt it fast, feverishly. Her gasp of delight is completely worth it.

"For better...for worse," she dutifully repeats.

"For richer, for poorer."

She nods—but stops as I raise the necklace with both hands again. Looks from the golden stone in it and then up to me. "For richer, for poorer."

"In sickness, in health."

"In sickness, in health."

I lift the chain over her head. Lower it with reverence, even faltering a little as I do. Even if we were at the Plaza Hotel, in front of three hundred people, decked in designer everything with Bruno Mars ready to sing us into the future, I probably wouldn't be as fucking nervous as I am this moment.

"Until death do us part."

Ella lifts her hair, allowing the tiger's eye to fall between her breasts. I follow its descent, dipping my head, before pressing my lips against the stone. She wraps her arms around me, pulling me close until the necklace and her heartbeat are a union against my ear. Only then does she rasp words in answer to mine.

"Circle without end. Joy without finish. Love without bounds." She brushes a kiss along the top of my head. "And heart...with its completion."

The closing words of an Arcadian wedding ceremony.

I slide my eyes closed. Let the words permeate me, meshing to every cell of me, breathing in all the air of me. Only then do I shift, burrowing tighter against her, my lowered head surrounded by her arms, my whole being bound to her spirit.

"*Amsek-tana*, Mishella DaLysse," I whisper into her skin.

She strokes my hair. Takes a deep breath, swelling her heartbeat into my ear. "I love you too, Cassian Cameron Jonathan."

Poundings at the door break us apart.

The bubble falls into pieces around us.

"Cassian!"

It's Samsyn.

It's time.

"No." Ella clutches me with a grip that shouldn't astound me but does. For several seconds, I let her. Wrap her in my arms too, savoring the silken warmth of her skin, even the thundering fury of her heartbeat. "No!"

I draw back until our foreheads and noses are pressed together. Struggle to capture her lips with a kiss that encompasses the fullness of my heart. Yeah, even now. *Especially* now.

"Armeau."

She shakes her head slowly—though does so with the strength of a tigress. "No," she repeats. "Dammit!"

"Come on, my love." I order my feet and legs to work again. Tug her up with me. "We'll have some time on the way to the airport, okay?"

As she stands, she glares like a child who broke open the piñata, only to be showered in chunks of coal. But as Samsyn thunders again at the door, my fiery sorceress bursts back to life. "*Va cock de Créacu*," she mutters, scrambling back into her leggings and sweater. "Some patience, my prince?"

I actually chuckle, albeit with a bitter edge, while shoving into my own clothes. Scrub one hand down my face and another through my hair while pacing across the room to the door—taking my fucking time about it, despite Syn beating like flying monkeys are at his back.

"Shit."

Not flying monkeys.

Monkey *suits.*

Still just as dingy and ill-fitting as I remember. Still draped on the two assholes I wasn't expecting to see for two more hours. And their fun GI Joe Club of armed operatives—who look just as ready with their weapons as they did this morning in the service lounge.

"Freeze, motherfucker!"

Yeah. *Really* ready.

And probably a little more pissed-off.

"Settle the hell down." McCree, magnanimous because he *can* be, waits for the soldiers to lower their barrels before sauntering a few steps forward. "Greetings once more, Mr. Court. Fancy meeting you here."

Samsyn snorts with such fury, I'm sure a few nearby bulls are missing gonads now. "I am sorry, arkami. They fucking figured it out."

McCree grunts. "Like it was hard?"

"Shut up, man." Reyes also comes forward. Gives me a businesslike once-over and earns himself points for it—if I were giving either of them points. "So...yeah. We 'fucking figured it out.' Put on some shoes and let's go, Court." He holds up a hand at McCree, backing it up with a pointed stare. "If you cooperate this time, we'll even do this without the cuffs."

McCree smirks. "Looks like he might've been enjoying some, anyway."

"I said shut *up*." Reyes swings his regard back to me. Shockingly, his expression edges toward an apology, though his voice remains the stuff of hardware store nail bins. "Say your goodbyes, get your shit, and let's go."

I'm smart enough to give him a respectful nod.

Then dumb enough to look once more to Mishella.

She's ghostly quiet—and just as white.

Still as a statue—and just as breathtaking.

I lift a hand to her face. Stare into her eyes—tearless now, thank God—but just as deep a torture with their watchful, powerful, incredible blue depths.

There's so much to say.

Yet nothing left to say at all.

So I step over, tuck her in tight, and whisper what's

easiest—for us both.

"You know what to do now."

Dammit. Easy isn't going to be on our side right now, either. Not when she answers with words that meant so much less than an hour ago—and remind me of the joy, the passion, and the completion I'm choosing, like the world's hugest dumb fuck, to walk away from.

"Yes, Cassian."

MISHELLA

You know what to do now.

I press shaking fingers to the curve of my ear, treasuring the vibration I swear is still there. Hearing his words, like echoes of the ocean in a seashell.

Hating myself for agreeing to them.

Knowing I have no choice but to obey.

If I am to trust he will fight as hard as he can against this slime bath of false accusations, I must uphold the promises I have made in return. To get on the plane. Let Laith fly me back to New York, and let Doyle return me to Temptation.

Where I shall pace new grooves of anxiety into Cassian Court's expensive carpets. Eat all the ice cream in his big fancy freezer to keep the stress at bay. Perhaps even let my "sweet parts" turn into wild tundras, since no entity except my vibrator shall have to forge that forest.

Except that the bonsun has already been talking of changing out the carpet.

And he hates ice cream.

And loves the hell out of my tundra, no matter how I groom it.

Damn him.

For being so utterly perfect.

For being so completely *not* here.

"Hey." Brooke's greeting breaks into my mope. The quiet concern in her eyes, about two shades lighter than mine, deletes any hope of hiding my misery from her—as if my swollen eyes, defeated shoulders, and twisted lips have not taken care of the job already. I am not sure I would find the energy for the deception anyway.

He is not dead.

He is just...gone.

It is all I can manage for a definition. The thought of him, so beautiful and noble and golden, surrounded by the squalor of Censhyr Prison, makes my stomach lurch to the point that I sink to the ottoman.

He will defeat this.

He is Cassian fucking Court.

He will defeat this.

Then he will go home. To Temptation. Where you will be waiting for him, in the middle of that worn carpet, with your wild forest girl parts and your arms wide open.

Ready to be filled by him once more.

Ready to become one with him once more.

But that is not accurate either. One touch of a hand to the golden stone at my throat is a perfect reminder of necessary correction.

Ready to *become* one with him?

No.

We are already one.

"Hey." I finally murmur it back, attempting to add a little smile at my friend. *Fail buzzer.* Even a weak pretense is not going to happen.

We hug, but the action is stiff. We do not try to fake that either. Things are simply not the same without Vy—though now that I have had a glimpse of the pain she must have endured in losing Alak, her resentful distance is easier to understand.

"You all set?" Brooke looks around the room, checking if I have left anything. "Of course, if I find anything, I can always ship it. Or just give to your par—" She darts an apologetic glance. "I'll just ship it."

"Thanks." I am listless, numb. Perhaps it will be possible to sleep on the plane, though on a couch in the main cabin—*not* in the bedroom now full of so many memories of Cassian.

And *that* will stop the thoughts of him?

He is everywhere...

And I do not want it any other way.

"Well then, the car's here." Brooke rolls her eyes. "We have to use one of the royal Bentleys, since all the Sprinters are still servicing the troops guarding the bridge."

Surprise, surprise. A real smile *does* bloom. "Goodness. Vy *is* going to be sad for missing the fun."

She embraces her own chance to laugh. "Right?"

As if our statements are two halves to a special spell, my phone chimes on the bed—with a photo identifier I do *not* expect. Near-black waves of silky hair. Impish grin next to fingers curved in the *ok* signal. Eyes of light orchid, shining during happier times for us. *Much* happier.

Brooke's jaw drops along with mine. It is taken over by her excited energy. "Wellll?"

"Well what?" It sounds as stunned as I feel.

"Aren't you going to see what she wants?"

Part of me—the girl in me—wants to say no. Vylet's evasion, while relatable, has been a salted nick since I arrived.

But another part of me—the woman I now embrace and appreciate, seeing more of myself through Cassian's eyes—yearns to simply love her, no strings or petty hurts attached. Today's events alone have slung some huge life lessons into the sack of my experience...

Along with one huge truth.

Every moment is a treasure.

And treasures are not given by the Creator to be wasted.

I walk to the bed, followed by a squee'ing Brooke, to scoop up my phone. After unlocking the home screen—a picture of a sundrenched Cassian from our sailing day on New York Harbor three weeks ago—I blink back tears at the familiar font of my best friend's text.

> *Heard about the mess with Cassian. I am sorry.*

Brooke gasps. "Halle-freaking-lujah. It's an olive branch, M!"

Quizzical glare. "Olive branches are for ending wars." My chest still panging from the image of Cassian, I add, "Or, in the case of Rune Kavill, for chopping off, sharpening up, and starting them."

A chest-deep growl rolls out of my friend. She follows with a spitted, "Amen," her own history with Kavill still clearly a fresh wound.

The little heart I sent as an answer receives a quick reply from Vy.

> *You staying here or heading back to NY?*

I tap back:

New York. Cassian has a legal team there, already working on things. These charges are the work of imbezaks.

I quickly add:

We are leaving for the airport now.

A strange instinct drives me to share it. Maybe a stupid hope—

Maybe you can stop by my place on your way.

—of that.

"Thank the Creator." Brooke breathes it while hugging me from behind. I smile once more but truly mean it this time.

"Let us be on our way, then."

At least *one* good thing will be coming from this trip to the airport.

★ ★ ★

Vylet has one of those rare situations most of us dream of. She and her sisters, Lauryl and Rynata, rent a house of their own along the south shore—but it is three doors away from their parents, affording the propriety still demanded by Arcadian society. Not that my friend worried too much about decorum once Alak proposed on New Year's Day. Everyone had been gathered for a big party on the beach. He pulled her away, up the shore a little—but not so far that we all could not see the man drop to his knees with a ring. Vy's answering scream had surely terrified even the fish. She had nearly ripped off the man's clothes in her haste to make the whole thing "official."

The two of them were beyond official.

They were the real thing.

A love story that inspired us all.

Proof that sometimes, the old ways still worked. That parents still cared—and got a girl one of the good ones. We were all told to look at Alak and Vy as an example of "young Arcadia's best"—everlasting love *because* of their parents, not in spite of them.

Nobody prepared us for an early end to everlasting.

A truth written across every plane of Vylet's face now.

I thought I had prepared myself. Knew the grief, now several days old, would gouge into her, perhaps fade her light a little. All right...maybe a lot.

Lauryl had answered the door and attempted to prepare us on our way out to the terrace. Muttered that she was glad Vy reached out, because she and Ryn had been scared. Brooke and I had traded a swift glance. *Scared?* Vy is a woman of many different moods, shades, and humors—but she is not scary.

Not before now.

Now...

I am scared.

The vibrant woman I have known for so long is...a skeleton. Beneath her sundress, a red pin-up style halter that is—*was*—one of Alak's favorites, her collarbones are prominent, her arms lifeless twigs. Her hair, once as lustrous as ink, is pulled into a dingy ponytail. Her skin is pale and splotched.

But her eyes...

are the worse part.

The brilliant centerpieces of her face, like bright-purple sparklers, were always the gateways to her infectious spirit, her take-no-shit humor, her easy and carefree laughter. They never just brought her name to life because of their color. They brought her essence to life because of *her*.

Her eyes now remind me of nothing but a grave.

The grave in which she has clearly buried herself, right alongside Alak.

"Vy." Somehow, it grates out. Unbelievably, without tears. I have only the Creator to thank for the restraint. He has given me a strange sixth sense for the day, telling me weeping will crumble this moment before it has begun.

"Shella-bean." Though it is just a rasp, she finishes it with a little croak—as if the endearment has become a very, *very* private joke. At my expense.

"Are you all r—"

Brooke shuts me down by stepping forward. "Merderim, my friend—for inviting us to stop by." Maybe that is for the best. Perhaps it is the years of crisis training she has logged with Samsyn's top lieutenants, or some of the social graces I drilled into her have paid off, but her words, followed with a sincere smile, seem to soften Vy.

Seem to.

"But of course." Soft has left the woman's vocabulary. The riposte is a social nicety brushed over her anger, as thin as poison on an enchanted apple. "I could not let you leave without a proper send-off." Her head swivels, looping her gaze out over the beach and the waves. The wind loosens tendrils of her hair across her gaunt cheekbones. "Saying goodbye is so important. *Every* time."

Brooke grabs the chance to look to me again. Jerks her head toward Vy, urging me to go forward again. I volley with a glare—*are you kidding?*—but she persists with a stubborn jab of her chin.

With a soft shuffle, I approach Vy again. "*Bonami*. Are you all right?"

She blinks rapidly. Scrapes the hair back from her face. For a second, my own eyes widen. Unlike everything else, her fingernails are perfectly groomed and polished. That is when I remember how much Alak loved her hands. Used to kiss her fingers, one by one...

"Goodbyes are important." Her repetition carries a new lilt. A strange one. But...a strong one. "You have to make them count, you know."

I dare another step closer to her. Softly say, "Yes. I do know."

She twists both hands into her wrinkled skirt, her posture stiffening as the wind picks up. "We hurried it," she intones. "Our goodbye. We rushed it like it was no big deal." Her head bobs, as if she silently orders herself to go on. "That day, when Prince Samsyn called and said he needed him...Alak ran for his go-pack, in such a rush. In five minutes, he was suited and out the door."

I reach out. Long to take her hand but grasp her shoulder instead. "I know—"

"Shut. *Up*."

She twists away. Stumbles back, hissing as if my hand is now the poison. Wipes at her shoulder before jerking her gaze up, finally looking straight at me. "You do *not* know, Mishella." Her face wavers. Her glass-thin composure starts to tremble, to dissolve. "You say you do, but you do not!"

"Then *talk to me*." I open my arms, letting the burn behind my eyes take over. Exposing my sorrow for everything she has lost...everything I want to help her get through, if I can. *If I can*. "Tell me, Vy. What do you need? What can I do?"

Of all the reactions in my expectations, her sudden laugh is not one. A laugh unlike any other I have ever heard from her—and I have listened to this woman laugh in a thousand ways—so high and shrill and hurting, it approaches a cackle. But not a gee-the-evil-enchantress-is-loony sound. It is the laugh of something darker. Harsher.

Scarier.

I look once more to Brooke. Her stance is tense and ready. Her eyes are observant and hard. She is thinking the exact same thing.

"What. Can. You. Do?" The verbal punches correspond to Vy's mechanical jerks back. "That is truly funny, my friend."

"Why?" I manage.

"Because you already did it." She strolls now, flitting her skirt, cocking her head. "Flew off to beautiful New York with your beautiful man, yes? Miss Cinder-*ella* of Arcadia, off to the ball in Manhattan, where you fell in love..."

"Vy." Brooke comes forward on her stealthy ninja steps. The observance does not add warm and fuzzies to my instinct about all this. "If you're going where I think you are, you can back off *right* now."

Vylet, still swishing the skirt, keeps advancing on me. Her lips do not surrender an inch of that tremulous, perilous smile. "You fell in love with him, Mishella...because he wanted you to. Because he wanted an ironclad *in* with the Arcadian court— and with all those juicy infrastructure opportunities."

"Vy..."

She waves Brooke off again. "He was *already* colluding with Kavill, right? He just needed someone stupid enough to jump on his Prince Charming *hook* and then let him ride her right into the core of our kingdom."

"Vy!" Brooke yells it now. "For shit sake!"

While I love my princess for her fury, I refuse to join it. The sixth sense is intense again, ordering me to stay focused, to consider my response—or even if I *should* answer. In the center of my mind's eye, a perfect apple blooms to life.

A poison apple.

Do not bite. Do not bite!

"I fell in love because I had no choice, Vy. Destiny did not give it to me."

Right into the middle of the orchard.

I do not care. I have no choice. Vylet has plunked Cassian into that orchard—and for him, I will walk into the mouth of hell.

At first, Vy says nothing. Actually appears ready for another hideous laugh, but instead opts for a small smile. A slow, savoring, confusing smile. "That so?" The matching murmur helps clear the fog. I have fed her exactly the words she wants. "Because he is your *soul mate*, right?" She inflects it in so many of the right places, it is clear she has rehearsed it. Has been waiting for exactly this moment. "Because he *knows you*?"

"Yes." *Shiny, pretty, poisoned fruit. Do. Not. Bite!* But I cannot let her continue—and she *will* continue—with conclusions she has twisted into the truth. The same fabricated lies the CIA found so easy to believe. "Yes. I fell in love with him for exactly those reasons—but for a thousand more as well." I fully face her, even imitating her pose. To someone walking on the sand, we probably look like a pair of players from one of the video games Cassian and Doyle enjoy playing—but like a Mei and a Mercy, will we be able to regenerate after this? Will our friendship? "He is an extraordinary man, Vy. Yes, he is driven and determined, tireless and at times even ruthless. He is uncompromising about excellence—most of all, from himself—and passionate about his loyalties." Firmed chin. Inflexible stare. The only ways to get through to her, it seems. "And yes, those loyalties now include Arcadia."

I wish her snort of a laugh came as a shock. Sadly, it does not—though now, it is no longer frightening either.

I only feel...

Sad.

Mourning deep for the friendship she is so willing to push aside in the name of targeting vengeance for Alak—proven clearly in her next sneered words.

"Oh, I am certain he *does* love Arcadia. And the zeroes in his bank account from it, as well."

For the first time *ever*, I have to mentally order myself not to slap her. "Cassian Court is *not* a murderer!"

Secretly, I hope *she* resorts to physicality. I would gladly endure a slap, even a punch, for any proof of the firecracker formerly known as Vylet Hester. But she reverts into a ghost again, canting her head toward me with unearthly interest. A zombie, eyeing its next delicious feast.

"He is a killer, Mishella."

Her whisper creeps into my very marrow. "You are *wrong*, Vy. You are so, so wrong!"

One side of her mouth quirks. Drops again—as her eyes thicken into dark-purple pools. "He killed my betranli."

"He killed nobody!"

"Be *quiet*, Brooke."

"It is the truth." I lunge, grabbing Vy again by the shoulder and compelling her to refocus on me. Why I am suddenly afraid for Brooke is a mystery I cannot ponder. Only taking action makes sense right now. "Cassian knew nothing about Kavill's plot. There is *proof.* I have seen it."

The little lip quirk again. Why is it more disturbing every time? "We are going to free you from him, Mishella."

Dear. Creator.

That is why.

I step back. Several inches to the right. Back toward the house.

Vy makes no move to follow—thank the saints. Not that I release a shred of my caution...my fear.

"*We*...who?"

Nothing like pinning down the crux of the issue.

Or feeling like complete hell when one's zombiefied best friend keeps staring as if she has already sprinkled one's brain with Tabasco.

Or finally understanding why, when our reunion party gains two new guests—pulling my breath up my throat in a dry, terrible choke.

"Holy fuck." Brooke's exclamation is strangled by rage and fear. Since I cannot phrase it any better, I let my mouth drop open, working to accommodate the screams of bewilderment and disappointment in my head.

Screams...

Colliding into one explicit message.

Run.

But I cannot.

The two figures behind Vylet, hands on her shoulders in a dual display of support, lock my feet down like titanium latches. I'm trapped. And paralyzed.

"Mother?" Agonizing gulp. "Father?"

As always, Maimanne is the one to speak first. "Bon

sabah, Mishella." She does not shift from Vy's side. Not a single muscle lifted to greet or embrace me. Her gaze, however, takes in every inch of my form, outfitted in a summer blouse and palazzo pants, purchased during a shopping trip with Kate in New York. "You look well." She dips a little nod toward Paipanne. "A little too...modern, I think."

"Surface details." For some reason, Father's perfunctory tone chills me more than Mother's. Though they are two peas in the same opportunistic pod, his bean has always peeked from the shell from time to time. Not today. Not at all. "A sow's ear can appear a fine purse, Selyna. We will at least make her look like a virgin again."

Instinct finally jolts again. Blasts the boots open. "You will not make me look like a damn thing."

This time, both sides of Vy's lips curl up. Some of the old spark dances across her face, but her teeth are a blatant clench, betraying how hard she works for it. "Shella-bean." Her attempt to soothe is just as forced and twice as frightening. "Come on. Everything is going to be fine. You are going to *thank* me—"

"Not if you are in league with them."

Fortitude arrives at my side in the form of Brooke. "There's nothing she wants from you anymore, Vy." She hooks my elbow with hers. "Nothing either of us wants." Her hold tightens. "Come on, M. We're bugging this nut farm."

"Mishella."

Paipanne calls it out, infused with just enough desperation to make me stop. But only for a moment.

"Goodbye, Father. Goodbye, Mother."

I am stunned yet empowered from the speaking of it. Like a rocket piercing the stratosphere, I am suddenly unbound from their gravity. *Weightless.* It is exhilarating...

And suddenly, extremely, over.

For a second, comprehension does not register. The pain in my neck is sharp, hot, excruciating. Have I been bitten by a mutant something? Has part of the building fallen on me? Have I been struck by lightning?

And then, I want to laugh.

Lightning. I actually thought of *that* as a possibility over the truth of this: a recognition burning my bloodstream deeper by the second. Filling my mind as my vision starts to blur, picking out the shape of Brooke's prone form, on the floor next to where I crumple, suddenly not weightless at all. Suddenly not anything at all.

Needle.

Needle.

Needle.

No.

No.

No!

I cling to the sound of my scream, if only in my mind, for as long as I can...

Before the darkness takes over.

CHAPTER NINE

CASSIAN

Dear fuck.

It's never been so good to be home.

Even Scott's goofy smile looks great. The guy races to greet the car, obviously tipped that I'd be arriving in Gabriel's Lexus. Though my attorney's black sedan is a work of art, it's not as flashy as the Jag or the Bimmers—and these days, I am *not* doing flashy.

Right now, the only thing I yearn to do is my woman.

Right. Fine. It's only been seven days. But I'm pretty damn certain that if Christ and Muhammad decided to physically roam the earth again, they'd choose forty days and nights in the desert again over a week in federal prison. Being separated from the place's general population after a day—the first of many signs proving my case was being eyeballed more closely, thanks to Gabriel's pressure—was little help for the questions that have swarmed me like pissed-off hornets.

Did she listen to me this time?

Did she get her ass onto the plane and then back here?

Has she been all right? Has she been sleeping? Eating? Thinking of me every two damn seconds, the way I've *been thinking of* her?

Common sense has tided me over with the most

comforting answers. I didn't let Reyes and McCree transport me from Arcadia without knowing she'd be looked after. Samsyn had been standing right there. I passed Doyle on the way out too. Brooke had probably personally gone with her, walked her all the way out onto the Sancti tarmac.

I still need to get out of this car—albeit with a new empathy for caged animals.

I itch for her like one of them, infested with a million fleas.

The second Gabe's driver fully brakes, I'm out. At once, attempt to do three things at once. Rejoice in my first breath of complete freedom. Return Scott's greeting with half a show of manners. Most importantly, bound for the stairs that will carry me to her.

A schism of disappointment hits when she doesn't appear there, waiting for me with those big blue eyes and that serene, loving smile. On the other hand, maybe she's waiting in our bed, wearing an even better smile and nothing else...

"Mr. Court." Scott extends his hand. "It's awesome to see you again, sir. Welcome home."

"Thanks, man." I accept the formality but start a frown. It's not that the kid never shook my hand before, only it's usually been without looking like we're at some high-society ball with two-by-fours up our asses. "Uh...everything okay?"

Scott averts his eyes—toward Gabriel. Something strange and silent passes between them. I follow the exchange, making sure the two of them know it.

"Cas." Gabriel takes over. Hits me with his courtroom stare. This exact look has brought him from not-a-chance to take-that-fuckers in many cases. "Let's talk."

"Talk?" I roll my eyes. Spit out a laugh. "All right, save your breath, barrister. You think I forgot the speech in less than an hour?" When he opens his mouth, I snap up a hand. "You got me out for home confinement until the Feds sift through the rest of their bullshit case. That means no leaving home, period." A wicked grin curls to my lips. "Believe me, that *isn't* going to be a problem."

Gabe's mouth forms a grim line. This is him, broadcasting my overshare. I smirk again. *This is me, not giving a fuck.*

"Now that I think about it, if you want to tell them you ordered me to *bed* confinement—"

"*Cas.*"

"What?"

He kicks the ground. Jams hands into his pockets. "It's about Mishella."

A warm wind, brought by twilight, blasts over the courtyard. At the edge of Labor Day weekend in New York, such a breeze is usually welcome by this time of the day.

Unless one's blood has already turned to ice.

"What about her?" I snarl it. I can't help it. He's just the designated messenger; I see that now. It was why Scott glanced to him in that mix of desperation and expectation. "And why the *hell* didn't you bring this up before now?"

I stamp the last word with fury. *The bastard.* I've seen him every day, sometimes twice a day, for the last goddamned week. We've been over every detail of this case—and the fact that the Feds don't have a goddamn leg to stand on, *because I'm innocent.*

None of that bullshit matters now.

The only reality that even counts is the one shredding my gut. The realization that she's not standing at the top of the stairs...

Because she's not here.

"Fuck." It breaks loose from my lips, mangled by my tight throat. Somehow, in some God-unknown way, I manage to keep the tears stuffed down. "What—what the *fuck* happened?"

Gabe exhales. Swipes a hand down his model-perfect face. Swoops that same hand around my shoulders before growling, "Let's go inside."

I let him lead me, at a loss for anything else. There's a deeper need to feed, too. Stepping off the elevator, into all the spaces that practically echo with her voice and her laughter and her light, brings a bizarre calmness. But like a hit of Ardbeg single malt, the buzz is temporary.

The only permanent high...is her.

I pull my head out of my morose ass long enough to smack a hug to Hodge, with gentler versions of the same for Prim and Mom. Their faces are pinched as tightly as Gabriel's, supplying me with more vital details.

Details that kick me at once into crisis-management mode.

That means getting my composure back online. And *that* means jamming my heart into a steel lock box and then swearing off on the key until Ella Santelle is back in my arms. It's the best way. The *only* way. I'm not going to figure any of this shit out by pulling a fetal rocking chair in the corner.

"All right." I lead the way into the living room. "Somebody's going to have to give it to me straight." I shoot a new stare straight for Gabe. Whether he likes it or not, group spokesperson seems to be his lot. "Well?" I demand. "What the fuck?"

"Cas." He unbuttons his suit jacket and sits.

"Wonderful. We've established you know my name." I give myself a silent clap on the back. Getting that out without openly inhaling one of the throw pillows, still imbued with her tropical vanilla scent, was no minor feat. "Now the rest, dammit." I lean both elbows on my knees. Gets me away from the pillows by a few inches more. "None of you had me sit down right away, so she's not dead. *Christ*"—a bitter shake of my head—"I actually had to start there."

The crack doesn't incite even half an eye roll from Gabe. Shit.

She's not dead. Take your goddamn blessing and roll with it from here.

A torment of a moment. Another.

Finally, Gabe utters, "She's still in Arcadia."

I mesh my fingers. Work the union tighter, twisting the webs at their bases. "All right." Look back up at him. "Did you assume she was elsewhere?"

"No." It turns some key inside him. With insolent grace, he leans back and crosses a leg. His gaze doesn't drop once. Neither does his brass. "There have been rumors, Cas. Fairly substantiated ones."

I grimace. "What the hell does *that* mean? What kind of rumors?"

Prim glances to Hodge. Receives a small, encouraging nod from him. "Cassian. This isn't easy—"

"What *kind* of rumors?" I lift the demand to a roar.

Gabriel doesn't flinch. But the brass tarnishes by a shade before he murmurs, "How...close...was your relationship with this woman?"

My teeth knock hard enough to vibrate my whole head. "*Close*, goddammit."

His regard grows lazy. A damn fine deception, but I see past it. I fucking invented it. "You were also paying for her time. Six months of it."

So much for the buzz.

I close my eyes. Push back the outrage threatening to take its place. *This isn't personal.* Gabe never makes things personal. By necessity, he knows about the original agreement with Ella. I have no idea if he even approves of it—he's paid well to keep such opinions to himself—and even now he brings it up as a fact, not an attack. But why?

"The contract was to take care of her, not me."

He snorts. "Clearly."

"Do you have a point?"

He recrosses his legs. Relevels his stare. "Think it would've developed into marriage?"

I push up until my knees buttress my palms. Never break eye contact with him, though my pulse slams pedal-to-metal from the images in my memory.

Ella kneeling with me, nude and tawny and breathtaking. Repeating promises back to me and finishing with her island's own sacred vow. The tiger's eye oval dropping between her breasts...over the heart she has just pledged to me.

"Yeah," I finally assert. "We would have—"

My voice clutches into silence.

My muscles freeze into paralysis.

As my senses seize in denial.

There have been rumors, Cas. Substantiated ones.

No.

Fuck, no.

"What. The. Hell?"

My shout shimmies the monitor mounted over the mantel. Now back on my feet, I whirl and stomp away before the urge to shatter it takes over.

Screw crisis-management mode. For that matter, screw its steel lockbox. Mentally, I yank the thing open—and smack my heart back out on my sleeve. What I can piece together of it.

Wisely, Gabriel keeps his seat. Doesn't stop his game face from dissolving or his stare from drifting to the bar. "You need a drink. *Fuck.*" He rises anyway. "*I* need a drink."

"I don't want a goddamn drink."

"Take the drink, Cassian."

Prim has a long list of no-bullshit tones, especially for me. The only time she ever used *this* one was over four years ago, after we buried her best friend...my wife. On that occasion, I'd been doing nothing *but* drinking. She'd handed me one more shot of Macallan and told me to enjoy the hell out of it—while tossing out every other drop of sauce in the house.

Before I can fathom what she means *this* time, she grabs the TV remote, clicking the monitor to life.

And makes me wonder if I really shouldn't have punched the thing.

Ella fills the screen.

She's radiant. Her hair is full and lustrous, her cheeks pink and rosy, her lips glossed and shiny...and smiling. A flowered dress with a scoop neck displays her cleavage to groan-inducing perfection.

The only thing hanging from her neck is a single strand of pearls.

The only other jewelry she wears is a ring on her left finger. A diamond ring...the size of a small goose egg.

My mind...

derails.

The remaining carnage of my heart slides in from my sleeve...

where it freezes...

hardens...

into a thousand knives, instantly turning in.

Scooping out everything that has ever made me whole.

Or human.

Or sane.

"What...the..."

I hear the words, but they aren't mine. How can they be, when my humanity has been stolen by the dark-haired, slimy-grinned shithead of a male now sitting in the Arcadian sun, next to the woman of *my* world?

Not just touching her.

Holding her.

Owning her.

Somebody else speaks now. A female. Not Prim or Mom. She's talking inside the screen. A newscaster of some sort.

"Earlier today, gossip 'net darling Mishella Santelle spoke exclusively to our cameras, to confirm the rumors *are* true. Tomorrow, she'll walk down the aisle to say 'I do,' Arcadian island style, with the Sancti Palais courtier who swept her off her feet in the wake of the island's Grand Sancti Bridge disaster. After everything the Arcadians have been through in the last week, the fairy tale nuptials will be a joyous celebration for all."

"Fuck."

Mom takes the snarl right out of my mouth. Not that the cotton replacing my spit will hand over anything but nausea right now.

"Zandyr Carris, the youngest member of Arcadia's High Council and a trusted advisor to King Evrest, has apparently received the full approval of Maimanne and Paipanne

Santelle—"

"I *bet* he has." The cotton gives me that much.

"—but it makes us all wonder: What about Cassian Court?"

The bile returns, twice as disgusting.

Mom takes her profanity to new levels of filth—and I gladly let her—as the program starts its "Cassian Loves Mishella" scrapbook.

"Wall Street's prince of passion returned from a whirlwind business trip to Arcadia just under two months ago, and destiny seemed to smile on his equally passionate pursuit of Mishella." The pictures cascade over the screen, from candid shots of our first outing together at the Literacy Ball to goofy pictures from our afternoon in Times Square, posing with the costumed crazies and indulging in tacky tourist food. "But was the 'Court'-ing just a smoke screen? Perhaps a way to make Demeter jealous? Was the Arcadian compelled to take action when she rushed back to the island—in Cassian's private jet, no less—after the successful terrorist attack on Sancti? And what does Cassian himself think about all this? Manhattan's eligible bachelorettes are eagerly awaiting the word, ready and willing to help the golden-haired god lick his wounds."

"Lick my..."

The syllables are harsh with fury. I rope the shit back by clenching a fist, though I'm unable to close the other. A tumbler of whiskey has somehow appeared in my hand. *A lot* of whiskey.

I hurl the glass against the wall.

Gabriel moves back. Smart man.

Prim and Mom surge forward. Not so smart. I brush them back, spreading my arms, while refocusing on the screen. The program has switched back to Ella and Demeter—and like the lovesick fuck I am, I need to listen.

To watch her.

And wonder.

Why?

Armeau.

Gift.

Raismette.

Reason.

Mine. Mine. Mine.

The refrain won't stop. Somehow, in some fucked-up way, I know it's true—even as I listen to her gush on and on about Zandyr.

How he loves making her tea in the morning...

"You drink *coffee* in the morning." I whisper it, reaching for her image.

How he rubs the back of her legs after they go running...

"You hate running. And your knees are ticklish."

How they like watching scary movies together...

"You hate horror more than you hate running."

By this point, I've joined every acne-covered fifteen-year-old in the pining losers' club. With my shoulders slumped and my gaze raised, I am nearly nose-to-nose with the bottom edge of the monitor.

And Prim steps up, standing right next to me. Her face is lifted too—but a different energy permeates her mien. An intensity...

No.

A worry.

I stare between her and the monitor. Even harder now, as she shoves her dreadlocks back with both hands. With fingers locked at the back of her head, she rasps, "Something's...not right."

The cotton in my mouth congeals into mud. Slowly, I nod. I think. I'm too wrapped up in looking at Ella.

In *looking* at her.

Radiance. It was my first impression when beholding her in the Arcadian sun, so damn far away. And the impression still applies...

To terrifying degrees.

Her gaze, usually darting a thousand directions, is fixated solely on the side of Demeter's neck. Her smile, always alive and quick as her wit, is pasted in a dreamy curve. Her posture, never surrendering an inch of dignity or regality, is an unthinking sideways slump.

No.

Not unthinking.

She's damn near unconscious.

"Holy. Shit." Prim nearly sobs it. I'm tempted to join her. Instead I lift both hands to the edge of the mantel and grip until my arms shake. Splinters come loose beneath my thumbs. The recognition hits us both at once. Like a goddamn kick to the ribs.

I finally force the words out. "She's completely spun."

"Out of her fucking mind."

"Huh?" Mom blurts.

"She's high," Prim supplies. "Fried. Baked. Tripping out."

"On...drugs?"

I flinch. There's no use telling her that treating the word like glass won't make it cut like a slab of the shit.

"*What?*" Gabe rushes forward, followed by Hodge. Gapes at the screen along with us. "God*damn*. You're right."

"Damn right I'm right." I haven't just seen this nightmare before. I've lived it. Watched it drive someone I love to suicide—right in front of my eyes. But Gabriel doesn't know that and never will. What he needs to know is exactly what I growl next. "*She* hasn't agreed to marry that buffoon at all. The drugs have."

He peers again at the monitor. Shakes his head in disbelief. "Can you tell what she's on?"

I move my shoulders in a shadow of a shrug. Rage prevents it from getting fully there. And disbelief. And despair. "Probably a cocktail," I grate. "Designed to make her look and act like the perfect, willing bride."

"Are you shitting me? Why? Who would do something like this?"

I push from the mantel, embracing the chance to form full fists. Propelling one of them through the monitor isn't an option anymore. I need to keep looking at the surreal evidence, supporting my answer. "Selyna and Fortin Santelle."

His eyes bug so wide, I actually see the dark brown in them. "Her *parents*?"

Mom sinks to the loveseat. Prim joins her, looking like I feel. Stunned. Afraid. Wondering what the fuck alternative universe we've just been thrust into.

I need to move. To do something. *Now*.

A march across the room takes me to the plastic bag of personal items returned to me on discharge from MCC. My phone is inside but dead; a week—hell, sometimes an hour—without recharge will do that to my device. I welcome the chance to rush to the home office and jam a charging cord into it.

I'm not sure what to feel about the frantic stream of texts

and voice mail alerts.

The texts are from Doyle.

Arcadia departure delayed. Ella didn't show up at the plane.

Ella's location unknown. Brooke missing too. On alert. Searching.

Girls still gone. Foul play suspected. Samsyn has called higher alert.

Brooke back. Fine and unharmed but can't remember shit. Ella still missing.

There's a delay in the messages. Two days' worth.

Insanity happening. Fuck fest of the worst degree. Laith and the plane have left; I've decided to stay. Where are you?

Another delay. One day.

Things beyond bizarre. Ella's at the Santelle villa; not accepting visitors. Fortin and Selyna up to fuckery. I feel it. CALL ME.

I burn to do just that. Force myself to tap on the voice mails first—all from Brooke. The first message is timestamped from four days ago.

Beep.

"Cassian? Ess Brooke Cimarron. Sorry for dah slurs. Still out of it a little. But you—you have to know wha's going on. Fortin...Selyna...they got to Vy. Used her as a decoy, to get us to stop on the way to the airport, then...then...*God...shit...* they drugged me, Cassian. Syn had the docs do tests. It was GHB, Cas. Liquid X, right into my neck. I—I don't remembah anything, until waking up back here. Mishella—she wasn't with me. We think those fuckers still have her. God, Cassian! I'm so scared—"

I end that call. My gut can't take the rest.

Beep.

"Cassian. Brooke again. Dammit; where *are* you? You didn't answer yesterday, so I'm assuming the legal red tape is thick. As soon as you get this, *call me.*"

Beep.

"Cassian, things have gone from bad to worse. Goddammit, they need to let you out, and you need to call me back—*as soon as possible.* Syn sent out a special recon team. They've confirmed the Santelles still have Mishella. They're—they're keeping her 'docile.' What does that even mean? *Call me* as soon as you get this."

Before pushing into the next beep, I rise and start to pace. Screw that. I start to stalk.

Beep.

"Cassian...if you don't get this soon, it's going to be too late. The Santelles made their move. Had their contract with you revoked, based on your arrest—and then immediately filed for a marriage license with the High Council. This asshole is *on* the High Council, so it was expedited and passed before the Cimarrons could blink. His name is Zandyr Carris, and he looks like a mobster with stock interest in Bryl Creem. Cassian—dammit—the wedding is day after tomorrow!"

I increase my pace. Battle the lust to crawl out of my skin

and turn into raw energy in order to transport to Arcadia this second.

The torment only worsens after the next tone.

Beep.

"Okay, forget calling me back. If you get this before Saturday, just put your ass back on a plane and get back here. *Please*, Cassian!"

I turn. Stab the button to disconnect the line. The hundred-plus other voice mails can wait. *Everything* else can wait.

Because nothing is more important than the call I activate now.

After one ring, a bewildered voice with a Duran Duran accent picks up. "Mr. Court?"

"Laith." I skip the normal banter about his cycling club, his boxing class, and his current level in *Overwatch*. "What's your twenty?"

"I can be at Teterboro in half an hour."

"Make it twenty. I need the flight plan logged and wings up before bottom of the hour."

"And if the plan isn't approved on Sancti's end?"

"Then make sure you pack the diving parachutes too."

"Aces." There's a smirk in his assenting accent—and I'm sure I hear him humming before he disconnects. "Hungry Like the Wolf."

Fucking perfect.

And now, a perfect match for the growl cutting across the room at me.

Gabriel, looking ready to pull a full wolf act in his own right, hurls a scathing glower. "Did...you...just..."

I open a drawer. Yank out a portable charger and then

switch my phone to the new tether. "Sure as hell did." I return the glare as he stomps into my path. "Gabe, I do *not* want to break your pretty face."

"Are you out of your damn mind?"

"Are you hard of hearing?" I jerk up both brows. Dig deep to find composure. Every mile between here and Arcadia is now like a huge abyss. The sooner I get out of here, even a few steps closer to getting back my sun, the better. "Get. Out. Of. My. Way."

Gabriel lets me shove past but catches me by a shoulder. Whirls me back around while muttering through a growl, "Are her parents really responsible for this bullshit?"

I compress my lips. "They make the Lannisters look like Ozzie and Harriet."

His own mouth tightens. His stare swings to the side, a mess of conflict. "Dammit, Cas."

I spread my arms. "I just have to go pick up a special sundry." *On an island in the middle of the Mediterranean.* "I'll be right back, honey. I promise."

Prim appears in the doorway. She still looks shell-shocked, but a smile tugs at her lips. It widens as Hodge steps up—and wraps arms around her from behind. *Well, well, well.*

She holds up a plastic bag. "I packed lemon bars. They're Ella's favorite too."

After dipping a soft kiss to her forehead, Hodge looks back up to me. "I'll meet you downstairs." Nods at the monitor around my ankle. "Disabling that will take about five to ten... depending on how rusty I am."

Prim drags a hand through his dark hair but keeps staring at me. "Bring her home safe, dork face."

"You bet your ass." I shoot another look between the two

of them, filled with a secondary message. *You two have some shit to tell me, don't you?*

They respond with knowing smiles, though that's all the moment allows before Gabe strides up again. "As your lawyer, I can't condone this."

I rock back on my heels, contemplating that for an extended second. "Hmmm."

He glowers harder. "Hmmm?"

"Then you're fired."

As I expected—and hoped—he breaks into a grin. "Took you fucking long enough." He wastes no time in making a break for the elevator, grabbing the lemon bars from Prim as he goes. "We're taking the Lexus to Teterboro. My driver knows the shortcuts."

MISHELLA

The world...is a big cloud.

No. A rainbow.

Perhaps a cloud *and* a rainbow. *Yes.* And they are best friends. Wait. There is a unicorn too. A cloud, a rainbow, and a unicorn. A perfect threesome.

The way Vy, Brooke, and I were.

Were.

Sadness sweeps in. I twist a fist into the white poof of my skirt, fighting it. Losing. "Sis-friend-hood. Where are you now?" I listen to the sigh, spoken by the stranger who is me but really is not, and struggle to keep a tear from spilling. *Oh, dear Creator. Do not cry! Maimanne will be furious!*

But I cannot help it.

Grief just feels...

right.

As if I *should* be feeling it.

Fear, as well. And worry. And loss. And stress. And all the other things that should be...*balancing* me...

Why?

Why does the cloud not have that answer for me?

Why does it feel so important all of a sudden?

"Oh, Mishella."

Maimanne.

When did she come back into my bedroom? And why is she clucking at me like that?

Tears. Oh, yes. Those.

Dammit. I have done it now. "Sorry, Maimanne. I was thinking of Vy and Brooke..." Suddenly, a thought blares in. It is alarming and—clear. *So clear.* And horrifying. And terrifying. "And Cassian," I jerk to my feet. "Oh my *Creator.* Cassian—"

"*Left.*" Mother brackets my shoulders, leaning her head forward and boring her gaze into me. "He left Arcadia, remember?" For a moment, a wonderful little moment, her eyes actually soften. "He left *you,* Mishella."

My chest clutches with pain. Awful, indefinable pain. My knees give out. I drop back to the chair, billowing out my big white dress. "Right. He left. Oh..." The last is just a whisper as the damn tears threaten again.

"Ssshhh, girl. It will be all right now." She kneels next to me, a black box in her hand. The magic box. I lock a longing gaze on it. "Stop all this nonsense. It is your wedding day, and you are beautiful."

I glare. Bare my teeth in a hiss. "I am a fucking marshmallow." Somebody—the other me—gasps in horror. Did I just really say that? And get away with it? Now I want to giggle—if only it would not tempt me so strongly to throw up. Why am I sweating so much too? And why do I want to keep thinking of Cassian? Because of all the delicious things it does to everything between my thighs?

I hate even considering those things with Zandyr. He looks at me like something to eat. Funny, since he smells like a kitchen. And hair cream.

But he loves me. Maimanne and Paipanne say so.

But I do not love him.

Why am I marrying him?

Cassian saved me from this. I went to New York with him, to be saved from this. And then he loved me. And I loved him back...

And then he left. Why? *Why?*

I cannot remember.

I need to remember.

No. You just need the magic black box.

Mother opens it with blessed speed. "You will feel better soon."

"Yes." I watch from hooded eyes as she fills one of the pretty vials and then briskly taps it with one finger. "I will feel better."

Give me the happiness.

Even if it is a lie.

Even if I know I must wake up soon and remember it is a lie. And finally remember why the *hell* Cassian left...

"Give me your hand."

His face fills my mind as I obey. The shape of it, so chiseled and noble. Tawny brows in his high forehead, sometimes mussed when he wakes from sleep. The dimples, which can be sharp with humor or soft with adoration. His mouth, confident and eloquent, the top like a sensual landscape, the bottom an enticing pillow.

I save his eyes for the last of it. As the needle pricks the skin between my middle fingers, I let them consume me. Fly me away into the vast, verdant wonder of them...the heated, lusting passion of them...all the passion and promise in them...

I let out my breath as the happiness seeps in. Mother rustles to her feet, but I do not say goodbye. It is lovely just to be alone with the happiness again...

With him.

"Cassian." The whisper echoes in the blissful blackness of my mind. I keep my eyes closed just a moment longer, imagining myself back in his arms, awash in his warmth, connected to his soul...lost in his love.

One more moment.

It is all I will allow myself. All I *can* allow.

"Ella."

And just like that, I break my own rule. *Just one more moment...*

But I can *hear* him now. Dear saints, I had forgotten the beauty of his baritone. I even smell him...not a kitchen at all. Cedar and sandalwood, leather and wind, twining into the threads of my being, fusing with the very center of my existence, making him my soul once more.

And then...

More.

Feeling him too. Quivering the air itself. Pulling on me, like the countering magnet to his.

"Ella!"

I squeeze my eyes harder. Selfishly seize another moment. *One. More. Moment!*

"*Ella. Christ.* Fuck! She's not responding. What the hell is wrong with her?"

I push my eyes open.

And am filled with him again.

Smile up at him, unafraid to let the tears flow now. If Mother wants a perfect marshmallow bride, she can summon the makeup artist again. But maybe she will not have to. Maybe...I am dying. Maybe she gave me too much of the happiness, and this is the juice finishing me.

Hmmm. Dying is not so bad after all.

"You are *not* authorized to say that again, woman."

His tormented croak brings my fingers to my lips. Did I say that out loud? And if I did, *am* I dying? What is real? What is going on? And why does the world swirl as Cassian hauls me up into his arms?

Oh.

His arms.

This...feels real.

And sublime. And perfect. So, so perfect...

"Armeau." He heats my neck with its fervent command. My body trembles with his possessive clutch.

I tilt my head up. Well, try to. "Are you...real?"

He grips me tighter. The marshmallow swishes. "Yeah, ma dinné. I'm real."

Blurted sob. *Messy.* I do not care. *This is good. This is right. At last.* "Thank the Creator."

"Think you can hang on to me tighter?"

I will hang on forever...

I loll my head back. Plunge it forward to kiss the side of his neck. Oh, but—mmmm—he tastes so good. *Looks* so good, in his black Henley and jeans. He is mine. *All mine.*

Between my greedy suckles, I husk against his skin, "Do I get a reward if I obey?"

"Damn." It is barely a breath. In a harsher mutter, over my head, he mutters, "How much of this shit do they have her on?"

"More than what we first saw." It is growled by another male. Too wry to be Damon; too social to be Doyle. "They probably had to up the dosage just to get her into...that thing."

I break into a giggle. Knowing exactly what the voice refers to...feels good. Sarcasm. The other part of me liked that. The first part of me, from before. The part that does not need the happiness.

But right now, I cling to the happiness.

Especially in the next moment.

"Créacu's mercy!" No confusion now. It is Maimanne—and she is *mad*. "What the bloody *hell* is—"

"No!" The scream is all mine. So is the death grip I curl around Cassian along with it. "No! Do not send me back to her, Cassian!"

"Not a fucking chance."

Maimanne sneers. I stare hard at her mouth. How can such pretty teeth be turned into such ugliness? "You have *no* say over this anymore, Court."

"No? Then throw me in jail, Selyna—and prepare to follow me right in."

Mother, still her dressing robe for the ceremony, manages to give me a new shiver with her smooth sneer. "*This* should be interesting."

"That's just what the CIA said—once I gave them full access to any and all records of my dealings with you and Fortin. It's been interesting reading for them. *Very* interesting."

She parts her ruby-red lips. Hisses so hard, I wonder if my

own mother is half-vampire. "We have covered every track! You are just as implicated as us!"

"But I'm not the one with ties back to the Pura movement."

The hiss dies. Her skin slowly approaches the stain on her lips. "You. Have. No. *Proof.*"

"You sure about that?" A man strides across the room, clean-cut and dark-eyed, from the depths of my walk-in closet. "Because the dark web can be a *very* fun candy store of covered tracks." Instantly, I know this is the source of the not-Doyle-and-not-Damon voice. The man carries himself like a peer to Cassian. A kind one. He carries a small box of things that make my chest ache again. A pearl hairbrush, a cell phone with a pink sparkly cover, a diamond cuff bracelet—

And a necklace with a tiger's eye stone.

For reasons I cannot explain, I am unable to look away from that necklace. It feeds me strength. Gives me courage. Yes...even enough to push closer against Cassian and speak clearly enough for Maimanne to hear.

"Get me out of here, Cassian. Please."

The pressure of his lips atop my head is all too brief—but still absolutely perfect. "It'll be my complete pleasure, ma dinné."

Mother huffs in time to his steady stomps. Past the fog of the happiness, I sense her following us along the hallway and down the main stairs. But only when we are halfway down does she speak again.

"Mishella DaLysse! If you depart this villa now, you little ungrateful slut, you shall be nothing to us! *Nothing!* Do you hear me?"

One we get to the entrance foyer, Cassian pauses. Slowly turns. Lifts a glare up to her that frightens me and takes my breath away, in the same inscrutable moment. "And that's different than how you've looked at her *before* now...in *what* way?"

Maimanne mutters something beneath her breath. I cannot make it out now, nor do I care to. As we turn again, she boosts her voice to a scream. "You are a kimfuk, Cassian Court!"

"Probably am." Cassian mutters it as he carries me into the sunshine. "But I'm the fucker who's never going to let you near this woman again."

CHAPTER TEN

CASSIAN

"Laith!" I yell it before I'm done climbing the stairs into the jet. "Fire this fucker up and get us out of Oz!"

With every step, I pray to God this production of a wedding gown doesn't send me—and by default, Ella—back down to the tarmac, headfirst. *Success*. Followed by Gabriel, I stumble into the main cabin—where a surprise awaits my girl in the form of the one Arcadian friend who *hasn't* lost her mind.

"Brooke?" Ella gasps it before squirming to her feet. She sways for a second and then falls into a crushing hug with the diminutive blond princess. "My bonami," she rasps through tears.

"My bonami." It's just as much a sob in return. They bend into each other, a perfect embodiment of friendship, gratitude, and girl power. I shoot a look over their heads at Gabriel, Damon, and Doyle—the triumvirate making up my "guy power." Not that I'd ever say it aloud to the fuckers. Within the next week, they'll each receive a package conveying my thanks—and love. For Doyle, the high-end headphones he's been craving. Gabe will get a bottle of Macallan 30-Year. Damon, the only one who's my brother by blood, is the only stumper—but now I actually hold out hope for the chance to find out. If he's really done with the CIA, maybe we can be done with the fourteen years I mourned his "death."

Things feel better already.

But it's not time to sing "We Are the Champions" yet. There's one more foe I've got to fight for this woman—perhaps the toughest battle of them all. At least the one that will wrench my soul apart the most.

The one I was too late to fight for Lily.

No. The one I'd ignored, pushed aside, denied—instead wanting my woman happy, peaceful, angelic...a lot like Ella looks right now. I'd been so blind. Ignorant. Arrogant. Thought she was so fulfilled like that, all the time, because of *me*.

Doyle steps over. As always, his features are enigmatic, though I know he's read and processed the dark turn of my own thoughts.

"She's going to be okay, Cas."

Jaw grind, the brutal version. "I know. I *know*," I emphasize when his gaze tightens. "I won't let her fall." *Or throw herself out a seventh-floor window while I watch.*

"*We* won't let her fall." He turns away from the girls to line up his gaze, the same color and texture as a steel girder, with mine. "Cas. You are not alone."

I order my head to stay upright—but am overruled. I hope Doyle understands, for he has no way of knowing what power he's invoked. That those are the exact words *Ella* gave to *me* the night of our first real "date" together, attending the Manhattan Literacy Ball. The night had started with our entwined bodies in the limo but ended with my ass on a paramedics' stretcher, three bullets in my gut.

But she'd been there when I woke up from the ensuing surgery.

You are not alone.

She'd been there through every minute, every hour, every damn day of my six-week recovery.

You are not alone.

Just like she'd been there, in every cell of my body and fiber of my soul, as I paced a cement cell in the Metropolitan Correctional Center for seven damn days.

You are not alone.

Now it's my turn to prove it to her.

Starting right now.

"Armeau." I run a gentle hand down her back. "I'm sorry. We have to get out of here before your parents toss spike strips onto the runway or something."

"They won't." Brooke whisks two fingers up with the solemnity of a Girl Scout. "I swear it to you, Cassian. I'm here to see my girl off"—she winks at Ella—"but also as an emissary for the Cimarrons. Even Evrest has had his eyes opened to the Santelles' shenanigans now."

Gabriel grunts. "Pretty difficult for a king to keep his head in the sand after his sister-in-law was roofied and then dumped back on the front porch."

Brooke throws him a side-eye and then grins back at me. "I like him."

Doyle snorts. "Don't encourage it."

"Shut up, peon." Gabe turns his cocky glower into a rogue's smirk. Extends his elbow toward Brooke. "I'm escorting a princess safely back to her native soil."

Doyle shakes his head. "Yeah. Down all fifteen steps."

The girls giggle while hugging out their goodbyes. Doyle and Gabe trade more shit talk. Sheez. It's almost like we're at a dinner party again. *Normal* again.

But we're not. And we won't be. Not for a while.

The thought gives me new determination. Quietly, I pull Ella a closer. Murmur into her ear, "Come on, raismette. Let's get you more comfortable." Because if my estimations are right about the "feel-good cocktail" her parents had her on, she'll likely start withdrawal before we land at Teterboro.

With that in mind, I close and lock the door as soon as I get her back into the bedroom.

I'm barely done and turned back around when the woman is on me like a monkey.

A hot, passionate, very high, very horny monkey.

And God help me, I love it.

For a moment—all right, maybe longer—I let her grab my hair, part my lips, plunge in her tongue, and ravage whatever else she wants. And damn...that starts to include a lot. Her grip on my scalp, digging to the point of pain. The other hand beneath my shirt, rubbing my nipples. Then both hands in my crotch, fondling me. *All* of me.

She moans and squeezes.

I groan and harden.

Dear *fuck*, she feels good. *So. Damn. Good.* Even through the miles of meringue in which she's trapped, her little squirms and writhes are beyond wild.

Holy. *Shit.*

No. Even wild isn't even the right word.

Insatiable. That might be better.

Voracious. Another good one.

Erotic. Illicit. Utterly, unspeakably fuckable. Yeah. I could expand my vocabulary to all of those right now too.

"Ella." As I grasp both her wrists, my cock starts listing the hundred ways it hates me. I order the bastard to shut up, curling her arms between our chests. "*Ella*. Stop. Armeau—"

She silences me with another kiss. Her lips are brazen, bold. Her hips are grinding, urgent.

"You came back."

She says it against my lips, all breath and need and urgent offering. *Shit.* I'm in trouble. Deep trouble. Mere thoughts of just her white lace *panties* have been the fantasies to nearly make me orgasm in my pants before; now she's covered in the stuff. It cups her breasts, perfectly offsetting her creamy skin. Rises in a wide V, barely covering her shoulders—an invitation to simply push the damn dress off. The buttons down her back are just ornaments. They hide a zipper...that ends past the lush swell of her ass.

"I'll always come back." Though I have to say it past locked teeth, I mean every word. Cup her face with equal intent, praying my love makes its way past the fog with so much of her in its grip. "Dammit, Ella. I'll come for you if it means sailing to the Antarctic."

Somehow, at least a little of it gets through. A sheen of tears turns her gaze from morning to twilight blue before they're slowly blinked away...

And my lust-filled little monkey returns in full force.

"Antarctica is not necessary." Her sultry smile is hypnotizing. Before I know it, her hands drop back to where they started. "I just want you to come here."

"Christ." I'm strangled from getting anything else out, bucking into her magical grip. "You *are* a sorceress."

"And you are my wizard." She laughs a little, stroking me so perfectly. *Knowing* me. "So why should we not...take out your wand...and cast a few spells?"

A bark of laughter escapes. I can't help it. At any other time, in any other place, she'd be three shades of crimson and hiding behind her fingers at a *suggestion* of the words. They're corny and dirty...

And awesome.

And not right.

"Baby..." I still her hands once more. "Listen. You've got a lot of chemicals in your body right now. They're making you say and do things—"

"Things I would not normally say and do?"

Her nose puckers. Holy crap, I've missed that.

"Well...things you wouldn't say—"

"Then let us not *say* anything else." She turns her hands beneath mine, freeing the tips of her fingers enough to taunt my crotch again. Her stare is seductive, enhanced by the smoke-colored makeup they made her slather on for the "big day" with Zandyr. "*Doing* can be just as much fun, yes?"

Fuck, yes.

God, no.

I steel my jaw. "Not when you're jacked on all this shit, favori. It's called taking advantage of the situation. Taking advantage of *you*."

She could whip out a hidden Taser gun—not an impossibility, given the dress—and jolt me less than she does with her long girl growl. "Well dammit, Cassian. Then we shall just say *I* am taking advantage of *you*, all right?"

Dear Christ.

Can't the little minx just be babbling and happy and high, instead of perky, practical, and sensible?

"*Cassian.*"

In my brood, I'd dropped my head. *Huge* mistake. During those three seconds, she's managed to reach back and slide her zipper down—allowing her to finally step free from the meringue.

No Taser gun.

Ordnance that's deadlier. Dear God, so much more lethal.

Her body, gleaming and gorgeous, is clad in the complete bridal package...

All.

White.

Lace.

"Fuck."

I'm shocked I'm capable of *that*. After I selfishly indulge a second—and probably a third and fourth—full stare of her, I likely won't be as lucky.

A strapless bra is perfectly fitted to the swells of her breasts, riding low enough to give a peek at the heaven of her areolas. Her panties can't really be called a "garment," consisting of tiny strings barely holding on to a triangle of sheer white, its lacy edges framing an erotic view of the tawny strip where her hottest passion lies. Layered atop that is a garter belt accented with blue bows, snapped into thigh-high stockings, also white, that all but order my gaze to worship the curves of her thighs, the bare curve of her ass.

"Fuck."

Well. Guess I've got at least one more surprise left in me.

Though I'm enticed—and terrified—to find out if *she's* got any more.

I *had* to go and give *that* idea some credence.

A gulp thuds down my throat as she moves one hand, slowly and knowingly, up the front of her torso. Like a snake charmer and her cobra, she rivets every ounce of my gaze to her graceful oval nails, sliding and circling, teasing and taunting. Circles around her belly button. Playful swirls over both her breasts, inching the bra a little lower, before extending up her neck and over her chin. Finally, her lips part and her teeth gleam, nipping erotically at the tip of her finger.

Then licking it.

"Fuck." I drag it into a tortured groan this time. Even so, I manage to add in a harsh bite, "Me."

Ella hitches the corners of her mouth up. "If you insist."

Before I can process that, she lowers that naughty finger. Hooks it into the front of my pants. Pulls on me hard enough to knock me off-balance, slamming into her and plunging us both onto the bed. She wastes no time there either, digging hands into my hair, all but commanding me to slice my mouth down upon hers.

She doesn't have to take the lead for long.

She's delicious.

Wet.

Wanton.

Perfect.

Then gasping against me.

Thrusting up to me.

Sliding legs over me.

And spreading them for me...

Holy. Fucking. Hell.

I've never been so grateful for pants.

Without them, I'd already be balls-deep inside her. Her adorable little mewls would be fuel for my deep, hard thrusts. And her breasts, finally bursting all the way out of the bra, would be the inspiration for my ultimate release.

Not. Going. To. Happen.

Not here. Not right now.

I can't do this with her. Not *to* her. Not while she's like this, literally not in her right mind, unable to know what she really wants.

But she really wants you. *Without that shit running a marathon in her bloodstream, she'd still be writhing and ready for you.*

But without the drugs, *she'd* be telling me that—from *her* heart, mind, and libido. This way, I become part of the violation—and God knows if, in the end, she'll have the clarity of memories to know the difference. I'll not be that monster, even if I'm the monster she's in love with.

Nothing, even indulging the carnal fantasy of her right now, is more important than her safety, her security, her ultimate happiness.

"Cassian."

And nobody said nobility was fucking easy. One more moan like that, making her nipples tighten and her whole body tremble, and I may really turn into a cautionary tale about messing around fully clothed with a goddess on horny juice.

"*Please.*"

Not another moan, thank fuck—but it gives me enough time to breathe deep, resyncing my head and calming my dick. Relieved whoosh back out. I need to keep my head here. *Both* of them. Whatever she's on—and during the flight over from New York, Gabe and I did hours of research and floated hundreds of theories about it—could wallop her with withdrawals in a few hours or at any second. Simply "lingering nearby" isn't an option for me this trip. I'm committed to being on her like fucking meringue on a cake.

Just not *in* her.

The internal pep talk made me forget her death grip on my head. Down I'm dragged again, meeting the renewed heat of her lips and tongue with heated desire. How have I forgotten how this woman loves to kiss? And how damn good she is at it?

We don't pull apart until we have to, huffing like horny kids, pawing each other everywhere. It's strange, but accepting that I won't be fucking her has made the rest so much more erotic and exciting. Perhaps a little illicit. Perhaps a lot.

There's just one catch.

Ella hasn't grasped the whole plan. Not like I haven't laid down the law about it, either.

Time for that to change.

Even as she lifts her hips once more...all but begging me to tear that fabric from her pussy and then bury my cock in its place. The revving growl of the engines, powering the plane to higher altitude, only enhances the energy in the air, likely jacking the effects of the drugs in her system.

"*Faisi vive Créacu*, Cassian." She rages it as I ease off the crux of her body, shifting my weight to one elbow. "Come back. *Come back.* I am nearly going mad!"

I lean my chest back over hers. Capture her lips in a searing, commanding mesh. "I'm not going anywhere, sweet woman."

"Bullshit." She tears at my hair with one hand, scratches at my chest with the other. One at a time I remove them, guiding her grip around the edge of the mattress. She growls, removing them at once. I fight the answering awakening between my legs—like everything there isn't buzzing on a thousand cups of sexual java already—as well as the enticed amazement. Goddamn. That joy juice has turned my sorceress into a saber-tooth tigress, and never have I yearned more to add "wildcat tamer" to my resumé.

"Keep. Them. *Down*." I trump her growl with a snarl while shoving her hands back into place.

"And if I do not?"

Slow, seductive smirk. "We'll be in the air for eight hours, armeau. I'm sure I can find ways to keep you frustrated for seven of them."

She doesn't move her arms.

She *does* accuse, "You would actually do it."

"With pleasure."

"Please do not."

I brush a bunch of strawberry curls off her forehead. Smile down into her gorgeous, glam-girl face.

Slide my touch lower.

"I'm going to give you what you need, Ella."

Then lower...

As my touch dips beneath the thin triangle, she moans. Quivers. Captures her lower lip in her teeth. "But—"

"But what?"

"I need *you*."

"You already have me." I stroke a finger into her dewy center. Another. Her heat and slickness surround me, soak me. "Everything I am, Mishella. Everything I own. Everything I dream and feel and love...and crave."

"Cassian. Oh Creator!"

Her sigh is pure music as her back arches.

"Spread wider for me, armeau."

She complies with a whimper, parting her legs a little more. Then even more as I shove aside the filmy panel over her pussy. I watch without blinking, needing the visual of watching her blossom for me. A hiss of satisfaction breaks free as the pink and coral beauty of her spreads and glistens, finally revealing the erect bud at her core.

"Ahhhh!"

I meet her scream with a savoring snarl, taken to an

ecstasy I never knew just from watching hers. The feeling of power that comes with it...*fucking intoxicating.* I ride the high without shame, rolling my body into every new stroke in her wetness, hyperaware of each tremor she gives in return. Every shake, every sigh, every fragrant drop of her arousal...

Her hands twist against the mattress. Her skin beads with sweat. Her pussy shivers beneath my fingers. "Fuck," she pants. "I...I need—"

"I know what you need, ma dinné." I lean over, capturing her gaze in mine. Locking her to every flame of the fire in mine. The blaze of my need for her. The depths of my love for her. "I'm going to give it to you. I *always* want to give it to you."

"But what about—what about you? *You* have needs too..."

She interrupts herself on a gulp as I break the pace of my strokes. Wets her lips as I tilt a challenging glance, complete with a cocked eyebrow. "You keeping count again, Ella?" I find her most sensitive nub again—and pinch it. "What have I said before about that shit?"

She cries out before seeing I really expect an answer. "You have said...no counting."

I reward her by licking the seam of her lips. Once more beginning my rhythmic rubs in her pussy. "Not while you're wide open and wet for me."

She shudders. Wobbles out a nod. "Y-Yes, Cassian."

I press in a little harder. Flick her clit faster. "And ready... to erupt for me."

"Oh. *Oh.* Yes, Cassian."

"And agreeing to come for me."

"*Yes*, Cassian!"

"Now, Ella. Give it to me. *Now*."

Her mouth falls open on a silent scream. Her body coils,

beautifully tensing. Her sex pulses, violent and perfect and hot, as it implodes for my questing fingers. I watch, transfixed, certain this sight should be included on some list beside the Northern Lights, the Patagonian hills, and lunar rainbows for pure jaw-dropping magnificence. *Never.* The Creator, clearly rewarding me for some miracle I performed in another life, has gifted me alone with the miracle of her—and now I'm determined to be damn selfish about the hoard.

Though I'll never keep it a secret from her.

For the rest of her life, this woman is going to know how completely, thoroughly, and utterly I cherish her, worship her, will protect her.

I just pray to that Creator—and any other deities He happens to be kicking it with—that I'll be up for all three as soon as her DTs kick in.

For now, she finally settles in my arms—and drops into a sound sleep. I manage to fold up the comforter around her, unwilling to disturb her any further than that. An intractable instinct tells me we'll both soon need our strength.

As the miles widen between us and Arcadia, I distance myself from all thoughts about the place. They'll be revisited later, when I have the energy for sorting out the good from the bad—and when I'm not treasuring every breath rising through Mishella's body like it's my own.

Because it is.

MISHELLA

I am alive.

The words are a quiet assurance in my head as I gaze over the rim of my coffee cup at New York's predawn skyline. For the first time, there is a tiny bite in the air, and the trees lining the Hudson have begun changing colors for the fall. I smile, a little excited. The idea of seasons is exciting and new; Arcadia is a world of few nuances in weather.

My heart squeezes. While I know I will see my native land again—missing the double royal wedding day will *not* be an option—I recognize that returning to Arcadia will never really feel like returning home again. So much has changed now.

I have changed now.

But I am alive.

Many times over the last two weeks—too many to count—I have barely wanted that statement to be truth. The process of detoxifying my body from Mother's and Father's "happy juice" has been a personal hell, gutting the limits of my body and the stretches of my mind. It has altered me physically...and emotionally. I have struggled to comprehend the depths of it and largely failed.

Time. Everyone keeps telling me I need time.

But sometimes, like now, there is too damn much of it.

Too much space in my mind...for the doubts and the fear.

Cassian has spared no expense on anything, of course. Dr. French, a renowned detox specialist, was flown in from Los Angeles before we even landed at Teterboro and is still residing in one of the guest rooms. The counselor for everything above my neck, whom I simply refer to as Renee, started coming as soon as I was physically able to handle it, perhaps ten days ago. There has also been a yoga teacher—really named Yogi—and a nutritionist named Bo, who has a booming laugh, arms the size of my thighs, and a recipe for the best banana smoothies in the city.

Every day, I am much better physically. A little better mentally.

But in the core of my heart, something is missing.

Someone missing.

In that awesome—and unnerving—way he has of showing up as if summoned by my thoughts, that person strolls across the terrace now. He has been working mostly from the home office but has a few meetings at Court Towers today, so a blinding white shirt, pinstripe vest, and matching slacks turn him into the epitome of lean, gorgeous CEO. His hair, a little longer than he usually keeps it, is tamed back from his face in product-covered waves, curling in dark-gold chunks against his collar. There is not a whisker on his chiseled jaw. Even his unruly eyebrows seem to be carefully groomed.

"Oh *my*, Mr. Court." I laugh softly. "You clean up well."

"Monkey suit's okay, hmmm?" He follows the crack by sipping from his own cup and then looking out over the city for himself. Greedily, I embrace the moment to indulge a long stare at him. The definition of his muscled shoulders. The sleek taper of his torso. The proud brace of his long legs. And oh yes, the perfect roundness of his backside.

Gah.

He steals the air from my body.

But he will not even come close to letting me show it.

I rush to get in a new sip from my mug—before he hears my sob.

But I am not fast enough to sneak in the swipes beneath my eyes.

"Ella?" He is a blur past the fuzz of my vision, splashing coffee as he plunks down his cup, hurries to my side, and sweeps up one of my hands. *Like a doddering uncle.* "Armeau?" At least he wraps his other arm around my shoulders, tucking me close. By the *saints*, he smells good. "What is it?" he murmurs into my hair. "Feeling blue again?"

One of the largest side effects of purging the happy sauce from my body has been mood swings. I know they are another reason why Cassian has gone from constant passion to perpetual concern—though he has practically relegated me to the damn curio shelves along with his glass sculpture pieces.

The result has been nothing short of maddening. How can I not adore him for protecting me?

And how can I not hate him for it?

Everything hits a spill point. And I let it dump. Use it to spin around and in, leaping onto his lap, straddling his body with my own...

Slamming my lips over his.

A grunt of shock erupts from him, but I consume that too. I continue, relentless and ravenous, sucking on the coffee-and-man taste of him. Do not stop until he finally groans, opens, and parries my passion with his own. He raises both arms, roping my body. Fists my T-shirt—even fiddle at the clasp of my bra. As we release but linger, nipping at lips and chins and noses, I gasp against his lips, "Do it. Please, Cassian...show me you still want me."

His frown is instant and intense. "*What?*"

"I am not having 'the blues,' all right?" I do not hide my indignation—or my despair. "Though certainly, I keep thinking your balls must be that color by now."

"Ella—"

"And yet you do *nothing* about it!" It is teary and dramatic, and I do not care anymore. "Then I read about how we must be breaking up, and how you are now back on the market, and every woman in the city—the damn country—is making their strategy to catch you, and—"

"Whoa." He grasps the back of my neck, jerking me down for a hard kiss. "Okay. Back up. *Not* literally." Commands my hips back into place with equal rule. "Look at me. Up *here*, Ella, not at my nose." His gaze is incredible, as deep green as the lingering summer leaves in the trees but as piercing and perfect as rare emeralds. "*What* have you been reading? And *where*?"

I shake my head. Like *that* helps. My eyes sting. My chin wobbles. "Stupid things," I mutter. "In even stupider places. I know better than to believe it all..."

"And you don't, right?" He drives in his grip to my upper thighs. "You know none of that bullshit is true. That we'll prove them all wrong too—but not a second before you've processed all this and are ready."

I nod. And mean it. "All right."

"No," he persists. "You're still not 'all right,' are you? What's *really* going on?"

I breathe in deep. Then again. Once more. This is...harder than I thought. In truth, I have known him only three months. Of course, in those twelve weeks, I watched him get shot, and he watched me be forced with drugs. He has shared the ugly grief of his past; I have bared the stark loneliness of mine. We have become best friends. We have become lovers. He has taken my virginity.

He has captured my heart.

He has earned my soul.

"Ella?" It is not a charge to be ignored.

I wet my lips. Spread my hands along his shoulders. Striations of muscle, mighty and magnificent as the sea cliffs from home, flex beneath my touch.

Home.

I inwardly repeat the word—stunned by its effect on me. More clearly, by the things it does *not* bring up. Like confusion. Or loss. Or conflict.

A new revelation takes their place.

This is home now.

He is home now.

If I can only make him understand...

"I cannot 'process' anything more, Cassian."

He stiffens. Seems confused, then resigned, and then determined. "We'll just...explore new methods, then. Maybe hypnotherapy or acupuncture. I'll send French back to LA today. We probably don't need him anymore. You're physically fine now, and—"

I push a whole hand over his mouth. Counter the effect with a soft smile. "I do not need alternative therapies." Before I remove my hand, I trace the elegant lines of his mouth with my fingertips. "I need...you."

Bewilderment sweeps his face again. "Me?"

"*You*, Cassian."

"But you have me." His frown deepens. "Fuck, Ella. *You have me.*"

Another slow breath out. More of trying to see him through a teary haze. "Then have *me*." Another realization strikes. Maybe I am trying to use words when only action will show him. "Touch me." I curl my hands around his. Guide them up my waist, over my ribs, and then atop my breasts. That simple action makes me shiver against him...unveil a stare of hunger and need to him. "*Show me* that you still need me."

The changes in him are subtle...not discernible to anyone who would not be looking. But I *am* looking—and rejoice in it all. The flare of his nostrils. The parting of his lips. The new fire in his eyes, alight with understanding.

Yes. He still wants me. Desires me.

More than that.

I am his home, too.

The joy of it bursts within, spearing fresh tears to my eyes...compelling me closer to him even before he tugs on one of my hands.

Even before he takes the other hand...

And slides something onto my ring finger.

Chirp of surprise. Gasp of astonishment.

Bigger—much bigger—cry of shock.

There are diamonds—*lots* of them—brilliant baguettes and shimmering squares fitted into each other on a tapered band, all arranged to show off the unique cut of the stone at the ring's very center.

A tiger's eye.

I gape at it. At him. At the ring again. Back at him.

The bonsun is grinning like the king of the damn jungle. "So is *this* what you meant...about showing you...?"

As I smack his shoulder, he dissolves into chuckles. As I grab his chiseled, wonderful jaw, preparing to kiss him, that laughter is vanquished by the applause and whistles bursting across the terrace.

Together, we look to the doorway. The faces there, every one of them, open the faucet of my tears even more. If Cassian is my home now, they are indeed the family vital to it. Prim, Mallory, Hodge, Doyle—now even Damon—are the wildly approving audience to the kiss Cassian bestows to the golden gem on my finger...and then to its match, hanging on the chain over my heart.

"Miss Santelle?"

"Yes, Mr. Court?"

"Are you free to discuss...an exclusive contract?"

"Hmmm." Coy head tilt—the kind that drives him crazy in all the good ways. "I suppose it depends on the terms."

"Ah. Yes. The terms. They're very...complex. It'll take us some time to get through them."

"How much time?"

He flexes his jaw, bringing out the sexiest versions of his dimples—and the craziest flips in my belly. "What are you doing the rest of your life?"

"I think I can clear my schedule."

No laugh this time. But he smiles, drenching me in the glory of his gaze, the magnificence of his presence, the strength of his love...pulling me so tight that our heartbeats mesh as the beams of the new day break over the city skyline. They are golden, brilliant ribbons of light, celebrating our survival, our connection, our future...

Our bold, beautiful love.

ALSO BY ANGEL PAYNE

Honor Bound:
Saved
Cuffed
Seduced
Wild
Wet
Hot
Masked
Mastered
Conquered
Ruled

Secrets of Stone Series:
No Prince Charming
No More Masquerade
No Perfect Princess
No Magic Moment
No Lucky Number
No Simple Sacrifice
No Broken Bond
No White Knight
No Longer Lost
No Curtian Call

Lords of Sin:
A Fire In Heaven
Promise of Your Touch
Redemption
Surrender of the Dawn
Tradewinds

**For a full list of Angel's other titles,
visit her at AngelPayne.com**

ABOUT ANGEL PAYNE

USA Today bestselling romance author Angel Payne loves to focus on high-heat romance starring memorable alpha men and the women who love them. She has numerous book series to her credit, including the action-packed Bolt Saga and Honor Bound series, Secrets of Stone series (with Victoria Blue), the intertwined Cimarron and Temptation Court series, the Suited for Sin series, and the Lords of Sin historicals, as well as several standalone titles.

Angel is a native Southern Californian, leading to her love of being in the outdoors, where she often reads and writes. She still lives in Southern California with her soul-mate husband and beautiful daughter, to whom she is a proud cosplay/culture con mom. Her passions also include whisky tasting, shoe shopping, and travel.

Visit her at AngelPayne.com